THE CHOSEN

To Jim
With much
Love,
Elizabeth
Valente

May 26, 2016

Enjoy!

The Marked Series

BOOK ONE
The Chosen

BOOK TWO
The Revealing

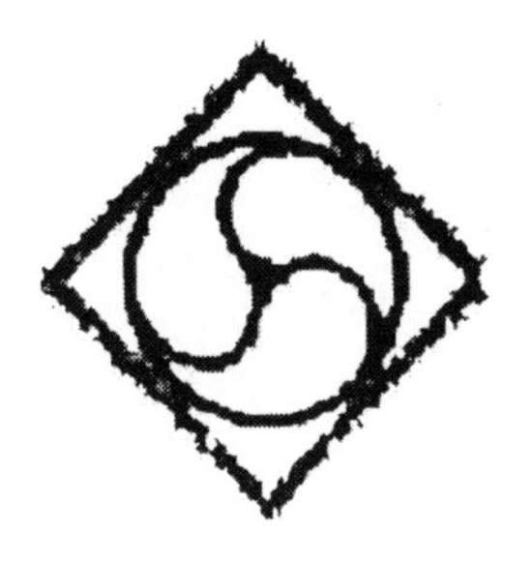

The Chosen
By Elizabeth Valente

Published by Woven Owl Publishing

Dedication

To Abby,
the person who stretches me farther than I could have ever imagined.
Thank you for teaching me joy.

To Jason,
my first reader and the one who told me I should finish what I'd started.
Thank you for always encouraging me and fostering my wild dreaming.

To Monica and Gloria,
my dazzling friends who lit a fire under me and got me going.
Thank you for your overwhelming support and praise.

A special thanks to:

Karyl Kartre, Susan, and Kristen,
for giving of your time and exceptional talents.
You both helped make this a reality.

My mom, Jessica, Kirstin, & Ylva,
for being generous with your time and praise.

TABLE OF CONTENTS

Prologue

Chapter 1

Chapter 2

Chapter 3

Chapter 4

Chapter 5

Chapter 6

Chapter 7

Chapter 8

Chapter 9

Chapter 10

Chapter 11

Chapter 12

Chapter 13

Chapter 14

Chapter 15

Chapter 16

Chapter 17

Chapter 18

Chapter 19

Chapter 20
Chapter 21
Chapter 22
Chapter 23
Chapter 24
Chapter 25
Chapter 26
Chapter 27
Chapter 28
Chapter 29
Chapter 30
Chapter 31
Chapter 32
Chapter 33
Chapter 34
Chapter 25
Chapter 36
Chapter 37
Chapter 38
Chapter 39
Chapter 40
Chapter 41

Chapter 42

Chapter 43

Chapter 44

Chapter 45

Chapter 46

Chapter 47

Chapter 48

Chapter 49

Chapter 50

Chapter 51

Chapter 52

Chapter 53

Chapter 54

Epilogue

About the Author

Prologue

The Chosen were always born on Days of Power - days when Nature's fury and potency could be transferred to those who would one day lead their people. It was those children who were catalogued and monitored - who were given the best of everything: training, education, and nutrition, while everyone waited for The Mark to appear. They were taken early from their parents, lest they be coddled, or even worse, raised by some ignorant country folk who did not know the ways of The Council. It was a great honor to have your child chosen. Were there not, after each Day of Power, lines of parents waiting to hand over their newborns, and even not-so-newborns? And yet there were still some that clung to the old ways. Therefore, years back The Council was forced to cast a wide net and take control of all births, so that none were lost. Even with all of their precautions, there came a day so forceful that it was beyond even *their* sphere of control – a day when several of The Chosen were lost.

CHAPTER 1
Max

Max took a moment to look out the darkened window. There were still no lights on in the city, the storm had blown them out and everything was eerily bathed in darkness. For a brief moment a flash of lightening illuminated everything and a movement to the right caught his eye. Mrs. Monroe was out with her miniature poodle, Daisy. The dog must be scared out of her wits, he thought. He needed to focus on that reminder that there were still things in this world that were normal and predictable, especially on this night.

A low moan pulled him from the window and back to Mara's side. He automatically grabbed the cloth soaking in the ceramic bowl by the bedside and wrung out the excess cool water. Max gently bathed her face and saw her try to rouse herself. Even by candlelight, he could clearly see she was exhausted.

"Please Mara, let me call the midwife. The storm is almost at its peak, there may not be any available soon." He knew it was useless, but he needed to ask.

"No," she whispered. "I....don't....want them to find her. They...can't know.... she was...born tonight."

"Shhhh," he soothed as he continued to bathe her face. He could see what an effort it took for her to speak. He knew how important this was to her, and he didn't want to upset her any more at this point. "I know, I know. They won't find her - I promise!" His next words were interrupted by a sudden crash of thunder.

He saw her face tense in anticipation of the next contraction. They'd had a blissful lull, but somehow he knew as the storm strengthened, so would the pain.

He'd prepared everything just as they'd planned; it seemed that tonight he would be helping to bring his daughter into the world whether he wanted to, or not.

"She's coming, Max," Mara said with a weak smile. "Our little one is coming." There was no more time for words as Mara bore down.

Max quickly became deaf to the storm raging outside, but the cries within would forever be imprinted on him.

CHAPTER 2

Anya
16 years later

Despite the ache in her leg and the tickle on her arm, Anya did not move. It seemed like hours that she had been crouched in that position, waiting for the right moment to spring. Her piercing silver eyes never left her prey while she calculated its next move. In unison Anya and the deer grew tense and alert to the sudden silence and stillness around them. Someone was coming. The faint creaking of an approaching wagon sent the deer bounding deeper into the brush, and a stab of disappointment streaking through Anya. Dinner was gone, but something stayed her departure. It was that same tug deep within her that she always obeyed when hunting - the mysterious knowing that always came before victory.

Anya could hear people talking, but she had to strain to make out what was being said. "They're sending a representative to the area." As they moved closer to her position she easily recognized the raspy voice of the old peddler who came to the village each month.

"Way out here? Why would they come out this far?" Anya didn't recognize the second voice, but knew that the peddler sometimes offered rides to travelers, for a small fee of course.

"Apparently, one of The Council is close to the end," and here there was a perceptible pause before the peddler continued in a hushed voice, "and The Mark has not yet appeared. The rumor is that none of the trainees are destined for The Council, that somehow The Chosen has slipped through their fingers and has gone all these years without detection."

"Impossible! Maybe it's a false alarm, maybe it isn't the end but a slight sickness, and that is why The Mark has not appeared."

The peddler reined in the horses, whether to give them a rest, or to better concentrate on his conversation Anya didn't know, but by now she too was completely drawn into what they were saying. For some reason she knew it was vitally important that she hear what was said next.

"That is what everyone thought at first, but he is not getting better, and more importantly the official Seer has foretold that it is the end. Everyone knows she is rarely wrong. Some in The Capital City are in a panic that the balance will be thrown off. That has never happened; it's common knowledge that balance is the key to The Council's success."

There was a pause in the conversation as the peddler adjusted the reins and made ready to continue on.

"Couldn't a Seer just tell everyone where to find The Chosen?" the stranger asked.

"No one can foretell where The Chosen is, not until The Mark fully appears, and even then they can't see an exact location. That's why they are sending scouts into all the Outlands, looking for missing Storm Children. It's their only chance." With that the peddler clicked his tongue and slapped the reins to continue on toward the village.

Once they were out of sight, Anya let go of the breath she hadn't realized she'd been holding in. She and her father had never stayed in one place long enough to go to any of the village schools. Her father had been the one who had taught her to read and to write. It was her father who had shared his vast knowledge of medicine and plants with her as she worked beside him. Now that she thought about it, she realized that he never talked much about The Capital City, much less the inner workings of the government. Being so far removed from it, Anya had never been curious about life in the city. It just hadn't seemed important, but now? Now, she had a sense that she needed to know, that somehow, it was vital that she understand what was happening there.

Anya was momentarily distracted from her thoughts by the burning ache in her right shoulder, and she absently brought her hand up to rub it. Over the last week, it had been steadily getting worse. It might be worth asking her father for some liniment or something, since it didn't seem to be going away on it's own. Thoughts of her father made her realize he would be waiting for her, and that it was time she was on her way.

As she arose from her position and gathered her things, she once again thought about what the peddler had said. They were sending scouts into the area to look for, what? "Storm Children" and someone called "The Chosen," he had said. What had he meant by that? This was yet another thing that she would have to ask her father about. She sighed and headed toward home, a little later and a lot lighter than she had hoped when she'd set out that morning.

CHAPTER 3

Conley

The knock on his door broke Conley's concentration, what little concentration he had left. He sighed deeply and put down the papers he had been looking at.

"Come in."

In walked Mrs. Martyn, his personal assistant, looking neat as a pin as usual. Her salt and pepper hair was pulled tightly back in its customary bun, and her navy skirt and sweater set spoke calmly of efficiency and professionalism. He would have been lost years ago without Mrs. Martyn. Wisdom was his talent, not organization.

"I'm sorry to interrupt, Sir, but these papers need your signature today." He could tell she didn't want to bother him at a time like this, but her practical nature had won out. Things would not run themselves.

"Yes, yes, of course. Not a problem, Mrs. Martyn. I could actually use a break from all of this reading." She crossed the room, not making a sound on the plush carpet and gently laid the papers in front of Conley. For several minutes the only sound was the periodic scratching of pen on paper as he reviewed and signed the necessary documents.

Once he was finished he gathered them back into a neat pile and handed them to her across the desk. "Thank you Mrs. Martyn." He caught her eye and saw the concern that was tempered there. "Thank you for everything. I don't tell you enough that I appreciate everything you do."

The concern seemed to deepen before she cleared her throat and regained her calm. "You're welcome, Sir."

He smiled as she turned and walked to the door. Mrs. Martyn was nothing if not predictable. He drew comfort in her unflappable façade. She closed the door softly behind her and he was once again left alone with his thoughts.

He sighed as he took off his glasses and placed them on the smooth wood of his enormous desk. He pinched the bridge of his nose, hoping that might relieve some of the tension that was edging toward a headache. There was still no word on Leander's condition. He was both comforted and disturbed by that fact.

Conley stood and turned to look out the wall of windows behind his desk. The whole of The Capital City spread before him, bathed in the glow of the setting sun. This was how he liked it the best, when the alabaster walls of the buildings were made softer by the warm tones of the day's end.

It was usually at this time of day that he grew maudlin and began thinking of the path his life had taken. Some days he could dismiss it, but lately it had been harder to resist. It always came back to one question: *Why him? Why was he chosen?* Of the thousands of people that could be standing in his position, why was he here? He had yet to find a satisfactory answer to that question.

Twenty-five years. It had been twenty-five years since his own mark had appeared and started him on this journey. He could barely remember the boy he once had been, and yet there were times when it seemed so clear, as if it were only yesterday.

***

25 years earlier

It was Visitation Day, the day when his parents came to the Center for their yearly visit with him. There was a part of him that wished they would stop coming, like many other parents did. They were basically strangers to him - as he was to them. He felt no connection with them or the five brothers and sisters that he had. They were all just far away faces in pictures. His parents tried; he would give them that. They even went so far as to send monthly letters detailing the family exploits. They would go on about his sister's first steps and first words, or his brothers' sporting events. He understood that it was their way of making him feel like he was a part of it all, like he was a member of their family. What they didn't understand is that those letters made him feel more alone and isolated than if they had cut communication altogether. Each line only served to remind him that he was not a part of who they were. He fully understood that these visits were for them. He suspected it eased their conscience; it assured them that they had done the right thing by giving him to the community so young.

He took extra care, as he got ready in the boys' dorm that morning. Despite everything, there was a part of him that wanted his parents to be proud and to know that he was flourishing. As he got out of the shower, he wrapped a thick towel around his waist and headed to the bank of sinks. He took a moment to gaze at the face he saw in the mirror, looking for some resemblance to those faces in the pictures. He knew he had his mother's deep brown eyes. People often told him that he had "old" eyes; he figured that was a nice way of saying he looked sad. The lower half of his face was definitely his father's, especially now that he was nearly an adult. His jawline had filled out and squared up, drawing more attention to the small cleft in his chin, and his nose was long and straight, hinting at aristocratic ancestors somewhere in his family history.

A sound outside the door shook him from his facial dissection and reminded him he didn't have much time. He grabbed a hand towel and scrubbed the excess water from his hair. He would need a haircut soon; he hated when it started to curl. He moved the towel to hug his neck and grabbed his shaving cream. As he made his first swipe with the razor, Max staggered in, disheveled and still half asleep.

Conley saw surprise on his face as Max realized he wasn't alone. "What are you doing up so early, Con?" he said around a yawn. "Did you forget it's Saturday?" Max groaned as he splashed some cool water on his face and scrubbed vigorously. "Wait. It *is* Saturday, right?" He looked up in panic and caught Conley's eye in the mirror.

Conley paused in his shaving to let out a small smile. Max was never any good before 9 a.m. "Yes, Max it is Saturday." He saw Max's relief before he continued; "It's also Visitation Day." He watched as the relief turned to sympathy. Max covered himself quickly, but it was not quick enough. Being an empathy talent, Max always had a hard time hiding his feelings, but he was getting better.

"Oh, right. Don't know how I missed that one." Max waited a beat and then continued. "Hey! Why don't we meet before afternoon training for a run?" A twinkle entered his eye as he continued, "We can run by the girls' dorm..."

The tightness that had taken hold in Conley's chest

began to loosen. "Yeah, that would be great. Thanks, man."

"Hey, you know me. I'm always up for showing off my manly form to the lady folk!" Max shot back as he puffed out his chest and flexed his scrawny arms.

Conley couldn't hold in the laugh as Max grabbed a towel and headed to the showers, whistling as he went.

That night was when the pain had started. Conley remembered thinking he had strained his shoulder during exercises that afternoon. It was a muscle pain that began deep within his right shoulder. It emerged as an ache when he moved, but after nearly a week of no relief he began to think it might not be something he could shake off.

It was on the seventh day that he awoke in the middle of the night to a searing pain on the surface of his skin. He remembered it so clearly because once he could focus his mind past the agony that had pulled him from sleep, he noticed that his clothes and sheets were soaked through with sweat. It was as if his whole body was on fire, but the white-hot burning was focused most intensely on a spot just above his right shoulder blade.

Once he felt sure he would be able to stand without fainting or throwing up, he swung his feet to the cool floor, grabbed his bedpost and pulled himself up. He looked around and noticed that his other roommates were sleeping peacefully, unaware of his suffering. Another stab of pain hit him out of nowhere, taking his breath away. His thoughts became consumed with quenching the fire that seemed to be engulfing him. He let go of the bedpost and staggered toward the door.

He started peeling off his clothes once he got into the bathroom and let them fall where they would. He was running by the time he got to the first shower stall.

He tore open the curtain and reached desperately for the handle of the faucet, turning it as far to the right as it would go. The ice-cold water hit him and he sighed in relief. The sting of the water pressure sent needles of pain along his skin, but it was nothing compared to the burning. He found that if he propped his hands against the wall of the shower and let the water hit his scalp, it would run down his body, soothing without stinging.

He didn't know how long he stood like that before the shivering started, but he was too exhausted to turn off the cold spray, and so he remained where he was. He probably would have stayed there until morning if it weren't for Max. Neither of them were ever quite sure what had pulled him from his sleep, but suddenly Max was there.

"Con, what the...?" Max reached in and turned off the spray. He quickly assessed the situation and got a couple of towels to wrap around Conley.

"Not...the...back," Conley gasped. "Don't touch my back."

Max seemed to understand as he led Conley to a bench where he could sit. He was so exhausted that he couldn't sit up straight and had to prop himself up with his forearms on his legs, leaving his back exposed to Max's view. It was then that he heard a sharp gasp from Max.

"My God, Con! Your back...it's...it's on your back!"

Conley half turned and saw the shock and fear in Max's eyes. Max started to back away from him, but stopped himself, knowing that Conley was starting to panic.

"What! What is it? What the hell is burning a hole through my back Max?"

"It looks like..." Max stopped and cleared his throat, "It looks like...*The Mark,"* he whispered.

That gave Conley enough energy to stand and get to the closest mirror. He quickly turned and looked at his reflection over his shoulder. There on his back, right below his shoulder were angry red welts in an unmistakable pattern. He could clearly see the circle with three swirling lines branching out from its center - all surrounded by a perfect square on its side. It was a symbol that he had seen before, in an ancient textbook years ago. It was *the* symbol, the symbol that marked him as one of The Chosen.

The ringing of the phone brought Conley back from the past. He reached across the papers on his desk and picked up the receiver.

"Yes?" he said, listening as Mrs. Martyn's efficient voice spoke into his ear. "Yes, put them through."

Conley listened intently to the person on the other end of the line while carefully sitting back in his chair. After several minutes he finally spoke. "Thank you doctor. I appreciate you letting me know. Please continue to keep me informed."

He replaced the receiver and gave himself a moment to digest the news he had just been given. With a heavy sigh he reached out and pressed the intercom button.

"Yes, Councilman Fitzgerald?"

"Mrs. Martyn, make the calls please. We will need to gather The Council. It is necessary that we be in Chambers within the hour. There is much that we need to discuss."

"Right away, sir," came the response.

He had no doubt that Mrs. Martyn would see to the necessary arrangements. For now he had to get started on constructing a plan; he had studied enough history to know that without a workable plan they were all headed toward disaster.

CHAPTER 4

Anya

Anya had expected to see some light inside the cabin as she approached it, but it was dark and still. Father must still be at the clinic in the village. Of all the places they'd lived, she loved this cabin the best. It was located on a small rise and almost completely surrounded by trees. The dark wood of the façade helped the house blend into its surroundings, making it almost invisible at certain points of the day. It was not a big cabin, but it was just right for the two of them. More house only meant more to clean. She loved her father dearly, but he wasn't the tidiest person, and often it was left to her to keep things in order. Her favorite part, though, was the front porch where she and her father would sit most evenings talking through their days or simply taking in the quiet of the night.

She figured she'd better get going on dinner, since it was more than likely that her father hadn't taken time for a decent lunch. She slipped her bow off her shoulder and automatically placed her leg between the wood and the string, using her weight as leverage to unstring the bow. She placed it carefully next to the front steps before removing her full quiver and resting it against the house. She paused to give her right shoulder a cautious roll, testing to see if the pain was still there. Halfway through she winced. Yep, she'd definitely have to ask her father about it. She sighed and turned her thoughts toward dinner. Giving one last mournful thought to the fresh meat that would not be on their table tonight, she opened the door and headed into the house, mentally inventorying their pantry as she went.

Her father arrived a little over an hour later as she

was setting out the dishes for dinner. She heard him depositing his belongings on the table just inside the door, a habit he'd gotten into long ago in order to be prepared for any emergencies that may arise during the night.

"I was beginning to wonder if you were ever coming home," Anya started to joke as she walked to the door to greet him. She stopped short, though, when she saw how tired and worn he was. She could see him trying to shake it off as he took a deep breath and attempted a smile.

"Yeah, there were a few moments when I wasn't so sure of that myself."

She knew from experience that he needed some time and normalcy before he would be ready to talk about what was upsetting him, so she deliberately lightened her tone. "Well, I think it's all part of your evil plan to get out of helping with dinner. You've timed it perfectly tonight. I just pulled the cornbread out of the oven, and the vegetable soup is all ready to go."

She could see the relief and thanks in his eyes as he walked toward her and planted a kiss on her forehead before throwing his arm across her shoulders. "Since I've worked so hard on my timing, we mustn't keep dinner waiting - it might throw everything off."

***

Tonight was definitely a "porch night." They both needed the quiet to review and digest their days. They'd had a pleasant dinner, talking about nonsense, both careful not to touch on any topics that might disrupt the cheery atmosphere. After dinner Father had even helped with the dishes, even though it was Anya's night. They sat for a time in silence, he in the ancient rocking chair and she on the porch steps, both enjoying the music of the woods around them.

"Mr. Collins had an accident at his shop today," her father began after a time. "Costa failed to secure the hobble on the horse Mr. Collins was shoeing," He continued with a sigh. "Collins took a hit to the temple before they were able to get the horse under control. Unless they get him to a Medical Center, he won't make it, and even then it's not guaranteed."

Anya didn't have to look at him to know how deeply he was troubled; she could hear it clearly in his voice. It was times like this when she wondered at his choice of professions. He was certainly excellent at what he did, and no matter how chaotic the situation he found himself in, he always kept his calm and knew just what to do. It was only when he wasn't able to save someone that his placid exterior faltered. He felt things so deeply; it was almost as if a part of him died along with his patient. Anya understood that right now he needed her to listen as he worked it out on his own.

"Costa should have known better. He may still be an apprentice, but he is well beyond a careless mistake like the one he made today." The frustration was evident in his voice. For a man as careful as her father was, there were no excuses for negligence. He took a deep breath and adjusted his position, as if a physical shift would help him shift his thoughts.

"So, I take it from the vegetable soup that your afternoon was not what you expected either?" he began.

Despite the reminder of her failure, Anya was thankful for the change in topics. "Ugh! I had it!" she exclaimed. "It was right there in front of me and I was ready to let the arrow fly, when the peddler came through and scared the deer away."

He let out a small noise letting her know that he

sympathized with her frustration.

"At least I was able to get a bit of gossip out of it," she continued.

A small chuckle escaped him. "Really? What did he have to say?"

Anya turned toward her father, excited to share what she'd heard. "He was talking about stuff that's going on in The Capital City." Anya began, not noticing the stillness that came over her father. "I guess one of The Council is sick - sick enough that he's close to death."

"Is that so? Did he happen to mention a name?" She could hear a faint tension creeping into his voice, but didn't understand why he would be concerned with a member of The Council way off in The Capital City.

"No...but he did say something about a mark." This time she couldn't miss the involuntary jerk of his head at the word "mark". There was no misunderstanding that her father definitely knew something about the mysterious symbol. "Supposedly, this mark hasn't appeared and they're going to be sending scouts into the area to look for missing talents, hoping to find someone called 'The Chosen'."

Fear was now written clearly across her father's face, which planted a pit somewhere deep within her stomach. She had never seen her father afraid. What had she said to cause that reaction?

"Dad?" she began tentatively. "Are you...is everything okay?" His eyes were directed on some point in the woods beyond, but that's not where his attention was. He looked as if he were lost in thought, seeing some distant memory.

"What? I'm sorry. What did you ask?" he said, as

his eyes focused again on her.

"What's going on?" Anya asked boldly. "What is all this about marks and scouts and 'Storm Children' and 'Chosen'? It obviously means something to you." Anya *knew* this was important and she needed answers.

Father let out a deep sigh. "Anya," he began in his most serious of tones, "I promise that I will tell you everything." He looked up and his promise was in his eyes. "Absolutely everything. You have my word. I just need a little more time. I need to organize my thoughts."

Oh, she wanted to argue, to demand he tell her everything before either of them moved from their spots. She was impatient to know what was so important that he had to "organize" his thinking, and yet there was a part of her that was fearful to hear what he had to tell her. Somehow she knew she would be different after knowing.

He never took his eyes off her as he waited for her to digest what he'd asked. Finally, she gave a tight nod, granting him the time he needed. She saw his small measure of relief that there would be no arguing tonight.

"Listen, why don't we take Friday afternoon and head out for a weekend in the woods? It would be nice to get away for a bit, wouldn't it?" He sounded so hopeful; she didn't have the heart to disagree.

"Yeah, sure. That would be great."

"Super! We'll head up to our favorite spot." And with that he let out a loud yawn that Anya wasn't completely convinced was quite authentic, and stood up, signaling the end of their evening. "Oh man, what a day. I'm completely beat."

Anya stood up, too, and made ready to head into the house.

Her father leaned over and gave her a kiss on the

top of her head and a gentle squeeze on her sore shoulder. She had decided during dinner that he didn't need one more thing to worry about tonight, so she wasn't even going to bring up the issue with her shoulder, but she flinched before she could even think about it.

He pulled back in surprised concern. "Anya?"

"Oh Dad, it's nothing," she said. "I think I just pulled something in my shoulder, or maybe it's just sore from sitting so long with my bow flexed. It's no biggie. I'm sure it will be fine in a few days."

"How long has it been hurting?" he asked.

"I don't know." She could tell he wasn't satisfied with that answer, so she added, "Maybe a couple of days? Three at the most - honest!" she added when she saw his skeptical look.

"Turn around and let me take a look at it," he ordered in his most doctorly tone.

"Dad! Honestly, it's fine," Anya said impatiently. "Really. I promise. It's nothing. If it still hurts tomorrow you can go all 'Super Doctor' on it." She could tell he wasn't totally convinced, but since she hadn't argued earlier, he'd let this one slide for her.

"Okay, but I won't forget to ask you about it in the morning," he warned, "first thing in the morning."

"Thanks, Dad. Good night," she said as she walked past him and opened the screen door.

"Good night, honey. I love you, Anya."

"I love you, too, Dad" was her automatic response. She turned and shot him a smile over her shoulder.

He responded with a genuine smile of his own. "I'll just make sure things are in order and locked up out here, then I'll be in for the night."

She watched him turn and walk down two steps to take his nightly walk around the property. He'd done that for as long as she could remember, part of his cautious nature, she supposed.

She let the screen door softly thump closed as she turned and walked through the darkened house to her bedroom. As she changed for bed, she continued to mull over the things that she'd heard today, and to wonder what she would learn this weekend. She pulled the covers back and slipped between the cool sheets. She climbed into bed and listened for the creak of the front door. Moments later she heard that telltale signal that meant her father was in for the night. As she closed her eyes she heard the soft rumble of thunder in the distance, a sound that always comforted her and lulled her gently to sleep.

***

The man watched from the woods until all the lights in the house were extinguished. He had been holding his position for several hours, since following the father back from the village, but he wasn't impatient to get moving. It's one of the traits that made him such a good scout, his ability to remain unperturbed with inactivity. He'd spent days observing the villagers and none of them stood out; they all fit naturally into the rustic settings that surrounded them. The rough tones of their speech were consistent with their coarse mannerisms, but those weren't the only indications that the majority of the villagers were born and raised here.

He'd learned early in his career that there were two types of people living in The Outlands. There were those who were born and raised here, the ones who rarely moved more than three houses down from where they were born. These were the people that dreamed while they were young about getting out and finding fame and fortune in The Capital City, but always found excuses why the time was not right. Eventually, those dreams were swallowed up by the hard work of surviving in this harsh land.

The other type of person in The Outlands was the one who was on the run or hiding from someone, or something. As hideouts go, The Outlands were perfect, if you could tolerate them. They would be where he would go if he ever needed to get lost. It wouldn't be difficult to copy the local dialect and imitate the manners of the region. The key, as he saw it, was not in changing your appearance, but in taking on the one trait of these Outlanders that would be the most difficult for someone with secrets: the penchant to talk.

When he began scouting he had expected the locals to be suspicious of him as a stranger among them. He realized almost immediately, and to his surprise, that instead of suspicion, he was greeted with anticipation. People couldn't wait to get at him and tell him their life stories. He was fresh meat, someone who didn't know everyone in town three generations back, and hadn't heard the local stories that had a way of gaining magnificence with each retelling. It was a subtle peculiarity of these people that someone who was trying hard to blend in, and fearful of being found, wouldn't notice, let alone strive to emulate.

Everyone that he came across in this village fit the mold, and he was ready to pack up and head on to the next town; that was until this morning's incident with the blacksmith. While the rest of the villagers were in a full-fledged panic, there was one person who kept his calm the whole time. It was clear to him that the doctor was a man who was no stranger to crisis. One did not get experience such as he displayed by living the life of a country doctor. This man was not from around here.

In order to test his theory, he made a point to talk with the doctor once he had the injured man stabilized. He tried every trick he could think of: small talk, flattery, he even fed him a personal story of his own. Nothing worked. He had listened politely and made all the right responses, but never dropped one nugget about himself or his family. That was when he had decided to follow the good doctor, in order to discover what he may be hiding.

There was certainly nothing out of the ordinary about the evening he had witnessed. He hadn't been close enough to hear what they were saying, but with the help of his spyglass he was able to get a good look at the young girl who was waiting for the doctor when he got home. It was evident that the girl was the man's daughter. Besides the doctor's clear paternal body language, she had the same thick dark hair and tall, lanky build as her father.

It didn't take him long to find a spot where he could sit and still have an unobstructed view of the house. He leaned his back against a strong oak tree, folded his arms across his chest, and closed his eyes. He guessed that if they were going to make a run for it, it wouldn't be until well past midnight, so he was good for a few hours of rest himself. He knew that word would soon reach them that scouts were in the area, so he was not going to let them out of his sight until he'd gotten their full story. All of his instincts told him there was more to the both of them than they wanted everyone to believe.

CHAPTER 5

Conley

Conley walked down the wide hallway that ended at the Secure Chamber where The Council met when discussing delicate matters of state. He paused before the heavy steel door and took a deep breath. He knew the others would be there soon so that together they could create a solution to the problem before them.

He reached out, pulled the door toward him, and crossed the threshold. The Secure Chamber was a smaller version of their regular meeting area. The room was dominated by a perfectly square mahogany table around which were four burgundy leather chairs, one for each member of The Council. Since it was important that the room remain safe, it didn't have any windows, but the lighting was such that it simulated natural light. Halfway up each of the walls was rich wood paneling, which had always made him feel as if he were in someone's library or personal study. They had recently updated the color of the upper half of the walls to a light taupe, which he much preferred over the dark hunter green that had been there for decades. Paintings by various artists covered the walls, the subjects of which were local landscapes. He suspected that was Mrs. Martyn's doing. Bringing the outside into this windowless room would be a detail that she would think of.

He walked over the soft Oriental rug to the table and placed his materials at his seat. He absently brushed his fingers over the brass nameplate on the back of his chair as he walked behind it to the buffet beyond.

Mrs. Martyn had indeed been busy. There was a full assortment of "brain food", as she would call it, laid before him. There was everything from fruit and nuts, to hard candy and chocolate. He bypassed the snacks and went right for the carafe of coffee. In mid-pour he heard the door open and turned to see a tall, regal looking woman in her 70s enter. Despite the late hour she looked fresh and completely coordinated in her plum-colored pantsuit and her designer brief case.

"Karis, thank you for coming on such short notice," Conley said.

"I've been expecting it for several days now," she replied as she placed her case on the floor next to her chair. As she straightened, the light shown off of her silver hair, which was neatly coiffed in a classic style that suited her perfectly. Conley took a moment to remember how she had intimidated him at their first meeting, and had to admit there was still a part of him that cowered when she regarded him with her penetrating blue eyes - even after all these years.

"Tea for you this evening?" Conley asked. "I can get it steeping for you if you would like."

"That would be lovely, thank you."

Conley made sure to grab the china cup and saucer that were always on hand for Karis's tea. She insisted that it didn't taste the same when drunk from one of the sturdy mugs that were provided for the others.

He heard her sigh before she said, "I suppose you're going to make me wait until Breanna gets here before you give me the details on Leander's condition."

"I should hope so," was the reply that came from the doorway. "You really don't want the poor man to have to repeat himself, do you Karis?"

Breanna was the only person he knew who could get away with talking that way to Karis. Then again, Breanna seemed to be able to get away with a lot of things others could not. She was a petite redhead in her late 30s who at first glance looked rather benign. He figured it was the guileless green eyes and the sprinkle of freckles across the bridge of her nose that made people assume that she could be easily dismissed. He had once heard her described as an iron rose; he always thought that was a perfect characterization. She had a soft beauty that drew people to her, but woe unto you if you underestimated her strength and determination.

He placed the tea at Karis's position and looked over at Breanna. "What can I pour for you?"

He saw her smile before she replied, "Well aren't you ever the gentleman? I'll just take a cup of that strong coffee Martyn always digs up from somewhere - plenty of cream and sugar, too, please."

"Of course," he replied and turned his back to prepare it for her. He heard the ladies making small talk as he took one more moment to gather his thoughts. He had several bombshells to drop tonight and he had to make sure they were timed perfectly.

He walked back to the table and placed Breanna's mug next to her right hand and continued on to the door. "Since we're all here," he paused for a moment thinking about Leander's absence, cleared his throat and continued, "I'll secure the door."

The heavy door closed with a soft whoosh and he slowly brought the lock down to prevent any unauthorized entrance. As many times as he had performed this task he never could shake the feeling that he wasn't so much as keeping the world out, but locking them in.

"Ladies? Shall we begin?"

CHAPTER 6

Anya

Friday arrived without further incident. Anya's shoulder still bothered her, but Father had looked at it the morning after their discussion and had not seen anything worrisome. He'd prescribed a regimen of ice and heat, along with some stretching exercises to loosen and strengthen the muscles. It wasn't helping as yet, but she knew that these things didn't go away overnight.

While Father went to the clinic, Anya spent the morning packing the necessary items for their weekend away. Her father had taught her very early on what was necessary to have and how to load her pack. He was always very insistent that she learn this skill, and that there was a right and wrong way to prepare.

"You always want the things you may need at a moment's notice around the edges," he'd told her as he opened up his pack to demonstrate. "Extra clothing, except for socks, are always at the bottom. You also want to make sure that the heavier items are placed in the middle. It will help you keep your balance and stave off blisters."

She'd watched with rapt interest as he filled the bag layer by layer, giving a detailed explanation as to why each item was more important than the next.

"And at the very top are your first aide supplies and socks."

She understood why the emergency equipment was of highest importance, but wasn't clear as to why socks warranted such high rank. She remembered letting out a laugh and asking what socks were doing with bandages.

He'd looked up at her and very seriously explained, "In the woods your feet become your most important physical asset. They are your transportation and in an emergency your instrument of escape. If you cannot walk, you may not survive." Somewhere along the way this lesson had been hammered into him, and he was now passing it on to her. "The last thing you need are blisters and sores from wet socks, therefore socks go on top in case you need a quick change mid-hike."

He had zipped up the pack and had her put it on so he could show her how she should balance the weight of it on her back. She recalled turning and seeing several items left on the floor. When she pointed out that he'd forgotten them, he'd instructed her that those were the things that she was to keep on her person at all times.

"Your pockets are for holding your knife, your compass, your flint, and your steel. Then your canteen gets clipped to your belt loop. If you ever get separated from your pack, these things will help you survive until you can get help."

She remembered thinking that this all seemed like an awful lot of stuff for a camping trip in the woods, but over time she came to accept it as necessary. It took several years before her father would trust her to pack everything correctly on her own, and even now she wasn't so sure he still didn't check things over before they left.

By the time he got home, she had everything ready to go. They had a quick bite to eat before locking everything up, hoisting their packs and heading out.

"Why don't we take the north trail?" her father asked. "It's a bit of a harder climb, but a much more interesting landscape, don't you think."

"I'm good with anything," Anya replied. For her this trip was less about the journey and more about the destination, or more importantly, the information she'd receive once they made camp.

It took them a good two hours to reach the spot where they would make camp, and then another hour was spent setting everything up and gathering supplies. Once Anya got the fire going, they unpacked a simple meal of pre-made sandwiches with celery and carrots. They generally brought their first meal when they went camping, knowing that the bulk of their time on the first evening would be devoted to set-up. Tomorrow they would go fishing in a nearby stream for their dinner.

Anya cleaned up the few remains of their meal, while her father set about hanging their extra rations. Once they had everything in order they both drew closer to the fire and settled in for the long conversation ahead.

She heard her father take a deep steadying breath before he began to speak. "First off, I want to say, thank you, for being so patient. I know that wasn't easy for you." He knew her so well. All day there had been moments when she'd had to stop herself from asking questions - it seemed like she had so many. Now that he was about to begin, though, there was a part of her that grew fearful and wanted to stop him from continuing.

"Secondly," and here he finally looked up at her, "I'm going to ask that you let me tell you the whole story, before you ask any questions. There is so much you need to know, and I don't want to leave anything out." At her nod he continued, "I will answer any questions you have once I'm done, but I need to get it all out at once."

She nodded again, bracing herself as he began.

"Before I begin our story, there are things that I must tell you in order for you to understand why your mother and I did what we did, and what has brought us to where we are today. This story actually begins over two hundred years ago in what is now The Capital City."

There was once a great king who ruled the countryside. He was a good king, strong and wise, and greatly loved by his people. Under his rule the kingdom prospered and there was great happiness. This king had two sons, Margrave and Raynor. Now, the laws of that time stated that the line of succession was through the oldest male heir, so Margrave was to be king once his father passed away.

The king loved both of his sons as any father would, but it was not a blind love; he could see their failings clearly. He knew that Margrave was power-hungry and selfish; he saw the cruel streak that ran through him and knew that it would not be good for his people if his elder son came into power.

Raynor, the younger son, was good and on the path to wisdom, but there was a weakness in him. He lacked the courage that it would take to fight his brother for the throne and make a strong leader.

The problem of who would lead his people caused many sleepless nights for the king, until finally one night he decided to go to the palace library in the hopes of finding some ancient wisdom that may help him find a solution. It was while he was in the library that a Spirit came to him and offered him an answer to the problems that had been haunting him - but it would be at a price.

The offer was this: Each year there would be a great storm in the city. A storm so powerful that Nature's energy would overflow. Any children born during this great Day of Power would be gifted with special talents and virtues. From those children, a Council of Four would be chosen. The Chosen would not always be the best and the brightest of The Storm Children, but instead they would be those who were the most needed for their time. It would be made clear who The Chosen were by a mark that would appear on them when the time was right. The symbol, or The Mark as it came to be known, consisted of a circle with three swirling lines radiating from its center - this was to signify the movement and eternal nature of time. The circle was enclosed by a perfect square positioned on its side. This was to symbolize stability, balance, direction and integrity. The Council would ensure that no one person had too much power, The Four would keep each other in check, and The Mark would guarantee power to the deserving.

This new plan, the king knew, would come at great personal sacrifice, for he was well aware of how important being king was to Margrave. He understood that such a deal would tear his family apart, but his mind won over his heart and he agreed to the Spirit's offer.

The next evening a great storm arrived in the city, the likes of which had never been seen. Booming thunder and powerful lightening were paired with forceful winds and sizable hail. The storm raged all night and was gone in the morning, leaving much destruction in its wake.

After ordering his troops to help the citizens repair the damage done to the city, he called his most trusted scribe to his chambers and had him write a full account of what had happened. He began with his midnight trip to the library and ended with an accounting of the storm's damage. He then swore the man to secrecy, on pain of death, for he knew that if word reached Margrave before

The Chosen were revealed their lives would be in jeopardy.

The king's next action was to send out a decree that all the children who were born the night before were to be brought to the palace in order to have his personal physicians check their health and well-being, never revealing that his real purpose was to find all those who were gifted by the storm.

Over the next few days, thirty-three families came to the palace with their newborn children. While each child was carefully examined and catalogued, the parents were given supplies and a stipend that was to go toward the care of their child. They were also given the directive to bring their child to the palace each year for an annual check-up.

Things continued in this way for the next 18 years. The great storms came to the city and the king would gather and catalog the children that were born during the storm. Soon it happened that the king himself became sick, he knew that his time was coming to an end. That year, when all of children gathered at the palace for their yearly physicals it was discovered that four of them had identical mysterious markings on their shoulders. The king was the only one not surprised by this.

He immediately gathered The Chosen together and read to them the account of his pact with the Spirit. He next assigned each one a protection detail, understanding that their very lives were now at risk. The Chosen began their training the very next day, for no one knew how much time the king had left.

As you can imagine, word spread quickly about the agreement, and the fact that Margrave was not to be king. Margrave had been suspicious for a while that his father never intended for him to inherit the throne, so he had been enlisting his own followers and gathering troops that were loyal to him.

A war ensued that lasted many months and culminated in a great battle, but despite Margrave's determination and cunning, he was no match for those who had been blessed by The Storms. It was during this war that the citizens of the city realized the rumors were true. The children who were born on a Day of Power were special and stood out among their peers. It was their wisdom, strategy, empathy, and leadership that had given them victory.

Suffering many losses and considerable humiliation, Margrave retreated to The Outlands and was not heard from again. Raynor, who had supported his father and had pledged his fidelity to The Council, was put in charge of developing the gifts and talents of the remaining Storm Children, who were now over 600 strong. The king and his people had seen that even though these children were not The Chosen, they were powerful assets and only served to make their city more formidable.

Eventually a training center was established where Storm Children were brought as infants and left by their parents to get specialized education and focused training. About once a generation The Mark would appear and that person would take his or her rightful place on The Council. The rest would grow to hold pivotal positions in government and society.

Here Father paused to get up and add some more wood to the fire. Anya hadn't even noticed that it had gotten so low, or that she had gotten so cold. She'd been completely engrossed by the story that her father had been weaving. After throwing a few branches on the fire, he brought her an extra blanket and wrapped it around her shoulders.

"So Dad?" Anya asked.

"Yes?" he replied as he once again took his seat near the mounting flames.

"You don't actually...um...believe all that stuff, do you?" she asked quietly. "I mean," she paused, "spirits and marks...and...and...Storm Children? That can't be possible." She looked at him, needing his reassurance that the whole story was just a strange legend that had grown more and more mystical as time had gone on.

She saw the half smile that broke out on his face, but the eyes he turned on her held only sadness. "If you would have asked me those questions when I was your age I would have told you with a great deal of confidence that there was no way any of this could be real. Like you, I supposed that it was all a bunch of nonsense, and only the most ignorant country bumpkins believed all that tripe about supernatural contracts and magical storms." He looked away and shook his head, saying almost to himself, "I was so arrogant and foolish."

"Then what...what made you change your mind?" Anya asked.

"That," he turned and gave her a full smile, the one that made him look years younger, "is where your mother comes in."

"My mother?" she asked in wonder. He never talked about her mother. She was almost afraid to move fearing he would stop.

"Yes, Anya your mother. She was the one that started me thinking there might be some truth to the stories. We met at The Center-"

"Wait!" Anya interrupted, "The Center? As in the "Training Center" in The Capital City?"

"Yes, the very same." Here he turned and caught her disbelieving eyes, "Anya, your mother and I were both Storm Children."

A small hiss of air left her lips, but she couldn't speak. She didn't know what to think, let alone what to say.

He gave her a moment to digest that before he continued. "We were born in the same year, and both came to The Center as infants, but that's where our similarities ended."

CHAPTER 7

Max
22 years earlier

Max secretly dreaded sparring days. He'd gladly take a good ten-mile run, or a survival hike in the woods over sparring. It wasn't so much that his build was not that of a warrior, he was strong and had the endurance of a good long-distance runner, he just didn't have the heart for fighting - even if it was only practice. He always did pretty well when he was on the defensive, but when it came to exploiting his opponents' weakness, and taking them down, he just couldn't do it. His matches usually ended with him flat on his back, looking up at the smug satisfaction of his opposition.

"Come on Max! If we don't hurry we'll be late to the field, and then we'll get laps for sure!" he heard Conley yell from the doorway.

And the downside to that would be? He thought, but he knew that Con lived for sparring days, and only enjoyed a run when he needed to blow off steam. Conley wasn't as tall as Max was, but he was stronger and quicker. It never mattered when his opponent had a longer reach than he did; he was so fast he was out of the way before anyone could land a strike. He saw Con's impatience to be out on the field, so he grabbed his shirt and slammed his locker shut. "All right, all right. I'm coming. I guess I'm due for a good butt whooping," he said. "It's been what? A whole week now since the last one?" he mumbled as he slipped his shirt over his head.

"Oh, come on now, it wasn't that bad." Con reassured him as they left the locker room. "Cheer up, maybe they'll let you spar with the girls today," he said with a wicked smile.

The fact that Conley didn't dodge Max's jab showed he felt bad about that last bit of ribbing, but all joking ended as they got closer to the field. A crowd had already gathered and the competitors were getting organized into pairs. They both broke into a jog and took their place in line.

***

"How is it possible that you look like you have *more* energy after one of these things, and I'm about to drop?" Max grumbled to Conley as they both headed back to the showers after the afternoon drills. As was typical, Max's muscles ached and he felt a mental exhaustion that went along with his physical fatigue. Not only was fighting not his "thing", being an empath, he had to work extra hard to block all of the emotions that were swirling around the practice field. Even though these were just drills, feelings still ran high and strong. Fear, rage and envy were always difficult for him to shut out, but when they came in large doses it was near to impossible. If he thought his body could take it, he would go for a nice long run to clear his mind, but he knew his limits.

Conley let out a hearty laugh and slapped Max on the shoulder. "Poor Max. You were doing great until it came to the quarterstaff. You've got to stay loose so you can move." Conley's words trailed off when he caught the glare that Max shot him.

"Oh, Crap! My quarterstaff." Max stopped walking and let out a sigh. "I left it at the field."

"I'll run down and get it." Conley offered. "You go hit the showers."

"No, I'll go. The quiet will do me good." He said as

he shot Conley a pointed look.

Conley smiled and put his hand on Max's shoulder. "Okay, I'll catch you at dinner."

Max watched Conley for a moment as he trotted off toward the locker rooms and let out a small smile. He could never stay mad at him. Shaking his head he turned and slowly made his way back to the field. To give himself more time he turned right and headed into the woods. He'd take the long way around and this would give him a chance to calm down and regain a measure of the peace he'd lost that morning. Everything about the woods worked like a balm on his agitated thoughts. He'd learned early on that the trees worked like a buffer, closing him off from the world and absorbing his distress. He'd always felt welcomed and protected by them, he was at home among them. He could feel his heart lighten, and, after a brief pause to inhale deeply the wonderful earthy smell surrounding him, he continued on.

Soon the back of the practice field was in sight. He remembered just where he'd left his quarterstaff and could spot it leaning lazily against a tree across the field. He was about to leave the shelter of the woods and cut across the dry dusty ground when something suddenly held him back. He'd been so deep in his own thoughts that he had failed to notice he wasn't the only one there.

He heard their voices before he saw them, but it was the man's harsh, angry voice that he latched on to first. "You continue to be a disgrace and a disappointment," he said. "Have I not continually told you how *vital* it is that you succeed? Have I not been clear enough for you?"

"Yes, sir," he heard a girl reply.

Max moved slowly in order to get a clear view of the two. He was careful to keep as much of his body hidden within the trees, knowing instinctively that it would not be good if he were discovered. The girl had her back to him, so all he could see was the long thick auburn braid that hung down her thin back. Something about the way she was standing made Max think he knew her, but before he could place her, his attention was drawn to the figure that loomed over her.

The man was tall with a powerful athletic build that was outfitted in the uniform of the Council Guard. His dark hair was closely cropped, but even so, Max could see the beginnings of gray near his temples. He had a face that many might consider handsome, with a straight nose and piercing gray eyes, but the mixture of disgust and contempt that contorted his features gave his countenance sinister overtones. Even without the many colorful badges displayed on his jacket Max could tell this was no mere underling. Everything about this man screamed rank and importance. He had to be one of the captains, but what was a high-ranking official doing on the practice field scolding one of the trainees? Officials never concerned themselves with a student's training. This was highly out of the ordinary.

"I had better see a marked improvement the next time I come to observe," the man warned. "I would hate for your lack of dedication to begin to affect others, wouldn't you?"

There was a slight stiffening of the girl's shoulders at the implied threat that she was just given. Max didn't understand the meaning, but clearly she did. He closed his eyes, zeroing in on her, and was immediately hit by a wave of fear. He could tell that she was desperately trying to get control of it so that she wouldn't show the man before her how much his words had affected her.

He instinctively sent calming thoughts her way to help her gain control. He opened his eyes to see the man trying to read her reaction.

"Do we have an understanding Mara?" he asked.

Mara! Yes, of course that's who the girl was. If Max hadn't been so distracted by the man he would have recognized her right away. Mara and he didn't share the same circle of friends, but he certainly knew who she was. In fact he wasn't sure if Mara had any friends at all, she always seemed to be on her own. Mara was known for doing everything perfectly. Some people assumed that she was arrogant and proud because instructors often singled her out to be an example. He'd always suspected that she hated the attention, but others didn't agree.

"Mara! Answer me." The man's sharp voice brought Max's attention back to the couple standing before him.

"Yes Sir," she said after a slight pause. "I understand."

The man shot one more warning look at her before he turned and marched off toward the cluster of buildings that was the Training Center. Max and the girl both watched him until he was beyond their sight. It was then that the girl released a long breath and let her shoulders slump. He could visibly see her let go of the control she had been hanging on to, and it was then that he clearly felt her weariness and the fear that surrounded her.

Without thinking about it Max made to move toward her. He must have made some small sound because the girl whipped around and peered into the woods behind her, freezing him in place.

"Who's there?" she demanded.

Max realized that because she was in the sunlight

she couldn't see him among the shadowy trees. He watched her scan the woods, seeking out what could have made the noise. He was about to give up and reveal himself when a small rabbit hopped past him and into the sunlight at the edge of the tree line. He watched as Mara looked down at the rabbit for a moment, and then back up to continue scanning the darkness in front of her.

"It's a good thing it's only you, little one," she said after a short time. On the surface it would seem that she was talking to the rabbit, but her attention never left the trees. "Bad things can happen to people who listen in on conversations that aren't their own. Some things are best forgotten."

Max clearly understood. There was nothing menacing about her bearing, there was no threat in the words, only warning. She knew that someone was there, and she was telling him or her that anything they had overheard could be dangerous to them.

The tension never left her body as she turned and headed toward the locker rooms. His eyes stayed glued to her form, in the hopes that by watching her his questions might be answered. He stayed where he was for quite some time replaying what he had heard and trying to look for answers that just weren't there. Finally, he sighed and went to retrieve his quarterstaff, being careful to keep to the shadowed edges of the forest.

***

"Did she ever find out that it was you in the woods?" Anya's soft question brought him back from the past with a start. He'd been so lost in his memories that he'd forgotten where he was. He stood and stretched the stiffness from his muscles before answering her.

"No. I never mentioned the episode to anyone," he sighed, "until now."

They were both silent for a bit, listening to the crackling of the burning wood and the night sounds that surrounded them. Anya was dying to ask so many questions, but knew that she had to tread carefully. She'd tried asking about her mother before, and he'd always avoided answering. Finally she'd stopped asking.

"In the weeks following what I'd seen and heard I watched Mara closely. I had never seen anyone with more determination, skill, and intelligence than she had. It seemed that whatever she did, she was the best. The more I watched her, the more fascinated I became with her. There was a part of me that needed to find out more about her, what made her tick." Anya saw her father's small smile as he remembered. "I was always quite shy with girls," he confessed as he met her eyes. "I must have racked my brain for days trying to figure out a way to start a conversation with her. In the end fate stepped in and offered me the perfect opportunity."

***

"Walsh!"

Max turned at the sound of his name to see the head medic poking his head out of the infirmary. He knew that look. There'd be no furlough for him this weekend. He turned back to his friends, "Look, you guys go on without me. If I can, I'll catch up later." They all knew that wouldn't be happening, but it was nice to think about.

He turned and headed back down the hallway. He opened the door and stepped into the controlled chaos of the Center's main medical facility. It seemed that he had been spending more and more time here lately. The powers that be had finally come to the realization that his talent was for healing wounds, not creating them.

"Change and scrub up, Walsh, we're going to need you tonight."

Max continued through triage and past examination stations to the staff lockers. Several months ago, they'd finally given him his own locker where he kept extras of everything for occasions just like this one.

After he'd changed and stowed his stuff, he met Dr. Archer at the scrub sink. "Apparently there was a particularly nasty training session. We should be getting a good half dozen trainees in the next few minutes. I've assigned you to rooms one through four. It's probably going to be a lot of wrapping wrists and ankles."

They both turned at the commotion that was beginning at the triage station. "Here we go, my boy!" Dr. Archer said with a pat on Max's shoulder. "Let me know if you need anything."

***

It had been a long afternoon and Max was exhausted. He was ready to head back to the dorms and crash, but he had one more patient to see. Things had gotten pretty crazy for a few hours, and now they had calmed down, his adrenaline was used up. Dr. Archer had looked even worse, so Max had told him that he could handle splinting the wrist of his last patient.

"I've got this, Doctor," Max told him. "You go home and I'll make sure things are closed up around here."

"Thanks, Walsh," Dr. Archer said. He paused for a moment and turned back to Max. "You've got the makings of an excellent physician, you know. I expect great things from you, son."

"Thanks, Doctor," Max felt a hot glow come to his cheeks at the unexpected praise. "Don't worry about a thing; I've got it covered."

Max turned and grabbed the chart that hung on exam room three not bothering to look at the name. "Well, it looks like it's just you and me," he started as he entered the room, but he trailed off when he realized who was waiting for him.

There in the corner chair sat Mara. She quietly raised her silver eyes to meet his shocked ones. He realized that he must look ridiculous standing there not saying anything when the polite inquiry in her eyes turned to confusion. He tried to cover his nervousness by looking down at her chart.

"Sorry," he cleared his throat and started again, "Sorry to keep you waiting. Things have been crazy out there."

"Not a problem," she said. "I was enjoying the peace and quiet."

"I'm Max - Maxwell Walsh, a third order medic here."

"Mara - Mara Evans," she said.

"Well, let's see what we've got here," he said as he sat down across from her.

"The doctor said nothing was broken - that it is just a bad sprain," she said as she lifted her arm onto the exam table.

He looked at the angry bruise and painful swelling on her delicate wrist. "Unfortunately, those are sometimes more painful than breaks, and they can take longer to heal too," Max said as he gently lifted her arm to take a closer look. "I'm sure he also told you that sometimes other injuries don't present themselves for a few days or weeks, so if this isn't feeling better soon, you should come back and let us take another look."

"Aren't you like, eighteen?" He looked up at her question. He saw genuine interest and curiosity in her eyes.

He smiled. "Seventeen, actually," he said. "I won't be eighteen for another month."

"Then how are you...?" she trailed off not sure how to ask what he was doing there.

Max stood up to get the splinting materials ready. "I was spending so much time here getting patched up after matches and training that they finally decided to put me to work." He turned to smile at her, "I'm much better at medicine than I am at fighting. You don't have to worry."

She sent a tentative smile back to him, and he was struck by how much that simple movement erased much of the seriousness from her face.

They chatted comfortably while he applied the splint and wound the bandage around her hand and arm. By the time he had finished he could have sworn he'd almost gotten a laugh out of her.

"Keep this on as much as you can and come back to see Dr. Archer in a couple of days," he told her as he stood up to clean up the exam room. "By then, the swelling will be down enough for him to make sure there isn't more serious damage. Let me get you your paperwork and the pain meds that Dr. Archer left. I'll be back in a few minutes." He left the room and sprinted back to his locker to get his stuff. He'd been handed this opportunity and he was going to take full advantage.

He came back into the room with his backpack slung over his shoulder. "Let's go," he said.

"Go where?"

"I'm walking you back to your dorm."

"Look," she started, "I'm totally fine. You don't have to do that."

He looked down at the paperwork in his hands and said, "I'm sorry it's part of the doctor's orders, and part of our service here." He looked up at her and gave her his best doctor face.

"Let me see," she demanded.

"I'm sorry?"

"Let me see where it says that - where the doctor wrote that."

"He wrote it on your chart that's on his desk," he said without missing a beat, "in his locked office." There was a moment of silence while she made her decision.

"You know I'm fine," she sighed. "You don't need to walk me back."

"I know I don't have to," he said as he grabbed her things, "but maybe I want to."

CHAPTER 8

Anya

Anya let out a long breath. It was hard to imagine her father as a boy her own age, flirting with a girl. She was hungry for more and could have sat there all night listening to stories, but as she looked over at him, she could see that letting those memories in had taken its toll. He looked haggard and somehow older than he had that morning.

"You know Dad, I think I'm going to call it a night," Anya said.

"Huh?" her father said as he was pulled from the past. "Oh, right. Yes, it is pretty late isn't it?"

"Yeah, you should get to sleep too."

"Yes, yes I will," he said as he turned back to the fire. "You go ahead and I'll just let the fire die out a bit more."

Anya walked over to him and placed a kiss on his crown, much like he used to do when she was younger. "Don't stay up too late, we've got fish to catch in the morning."

He smiled faintly and nodded, "You're right. I've got a record to break, don't I?"

"Ha!" Anya laughed, "As if you are any match for me." As long as she could remember, they'd had fishing contests to see who could catch the most fish. The loser was doomed to a night of hard labor, washing the dinner dishes, a chore they both hated with a passion. She hadn't had to do dishes in years, a fact that she ribbed him about often.

Anya walked over to her tent, took her shoes off, and bent to enter.

"I love you Anya," she heard her father say.

She paused and turned back to him. "I love you, too, Dad." She watched him for a moment more and then crawled into her shelter and between the folds of her sleeping bag. She figured with all she'd learned today she would have a hard time going to sleep, but she was more exhausted than she realized. She was asleep within moments, dreaming of far away kingdoms, angry princes, and Storm Spirits.

***

It looked like story time was over for now. The girl had gone to bed and the doctor sat staring into the flames, lost in his own thoughts. He hadn't been close enough to hear what they were saying, but he could tell by the looks on their faces that they were having a serious conversation. He would learn their secrets eventually. For now it was enough that he kept them in his sights. The more he watched them, the more his instincts told him these two were important.

He watched the man get up some time later and circle the camp, pausing periodically to listen intently - making sure he heard the night sounds that were supposed to be there. The doctor paused briefly and turned his head, peering intently into the darkness that hid him so well. The scout knew that he was nearly invisible, but his heart still skipped a few beats. The doctor moved on after a moment and he let out a soft breath. He didn't relax his muscles until the doctor had doused the flames of the fire and gone into his own tent. Only then did the scout sit down and settle in for the night, still keeping an eye on the doctor's tent. Oh yes, these two were valuable. He knew it. He allowed himself a small smile thinking of the reward The General would give for the pair before he closed his eyes to get an hour or two of sleep. Tomorrow would be another day of observation and then he'd begin planning. He had to be sure of their weaknesses before he set his trap.

CHAPTER 9

Conley

Conley shifted in his chair and pinched the bridge of his nose in a vain attempt to stave off the headache he knew was coming. They'd been going around and around his plan for over an hour, and he was ready to call it a night.

"Look," Breanna was saying, "I'm all for bending rules, heck I'm even for breaking them from time to time, but I just don't think this is one we should mess around with. When the time is right The Chosen will be revealed, it isn't our place to push it."

"I understand Conley's point though," Karis said after a brief pause, "we can't be the only ones looking for Leander's replacement. If whoever is targeting us thinks we've found The Chosen One, they'll back off their search."

"We're not even sure someone is targeting us." Breanna shot back.

"I'm sorry to say we are," Conley broke in. Both women turned to him waiting for him to offer his proof. "I got the call from the doctors this afternoon. Here is a copy of Leander's official report." He handed each of them a paper from his file folder. "As you see he had extremely high levels of potassium chloride in his system. If it wasn't standard protocol that whenever a member of The Council is admitted to the hospital a full battery of tests are run, it never would have been detected." He let that sink in before he continued. "The overdose caused cardiac arrest. If his wife hadn't gotten home when she did, he wouldn't be alive now."

The room was silent for several minutes. It was

Karis who finally spoke, "So what measures have you already taken?"

Despite the seriousness of the subject he had to smile; Karis knew him well. "I have several of the most trusted guards looking into possible suspects. At this point, everyone close to him is being examined."

"Even us?" Breanna asked in surprise.

"Of course we would be considered," Karis calmly stated as her eyes stayed firmly fixed on Conley.

"But what would we gain by his death?" Breanna asked. "We have no motive."

"It is only a formality," Conley cut in. "I've already given my statement and an account of my whereabouts for the hours before his attack. You both will be asked to do the same."

"Do they have any other, more plausible suspects?" Karis's question dripped with derision. Conley sensed her impatience, but understood its root. No matter what Karis wanted others to think, she did care - and care deeply. He saw the worry in her eyes and the need to find the person who was responsible for her friend's eminent death.

"They will of course start with his wife -" Conley began.

"Meredith had nothing to do with this!" Breanna cut in. Where Karis's anger was chill and cold, Breanna's was hot and volatile. You always knew where you stood with Breanna, and in a situation like this she would be the first to vehemently come to a friend's defense.

"We know that Bree." Conley deliberately spoke slowly and softly. "Again, it is just a formality."

"With all these 'formalities' it's a wonder they will have any time at all to look for the real culprit," Breanna shot back peevishly.

"They are also going over all his correspondence and interviewing any and all staff, hoping to compile a list of potential threats." Conley understood her impatience, for he felt the same, but his logic overruled his heart and he knew it would just take time. He straightened in his chair and continued, "Our security details will be increased. Even so, I would caution you both to be hyper-vigilant. Until we get this sorted out, keep only your most trusted friends and family around you."

He expected an argument from Karis on increased security, so he was slightly surprised at her next question. "Won't this plan of yours make us more of a target?"

"That is a distinct possibility," Conley calmly stated. He wasn't going to sugarcoat it; they needed to be aware of the personal risks involved if they decided to go ahead with the plan before them.

"And the young replacement?" Karis continued. "Will he or she understand the risk?"

This was the question Conley had asked himself over and over since the plan began to take shape in his mind. It was one thing to risk the lives of those who were already chosen. When The Mark appeared, the matter of safety and risk was answered for you. You had no choice in the matter. He'd often wondered if he'd had a choice, would he have elected to be a part of this Council? But to bring someone in, someone young and inexperienced, who wasn't chosen, would it be fair to them? He had no answer.

"They will be fully briefed on every risk, but you and I both know that a full understanding doesn't come until the position is taken." He had no other reassurances to give her. Part of the risk that they all had to be aware of was that they might end up with innocent blood on their hands.

"Do they have any potential candidates?" Bree asked as the full weight of what could happen was before them.

"I have asked Captain Hawkins to quietly compile a list," Conley replied, "The fewer that know anything the better, and I trust him to be discrete." Conley knew his plan hinged on finding the right person. This young man or woman would need to have the ability to lie convincingly to all of those closest to them by posing as the newest Chosen. At the same time, it was vital that they have the strength of character to step down from The Council once the real Chosen was finally found. Conley knew all too well that this person would be difficult to find. It was a gamble for everyone. The Council would be putting trust and faith in one who was untested, and this person would be expected to carry a mighty load - with no guarantees on how, or when, it would end. They just needed to buy themselves some time, and after days of thinking this was the only way Conley could think of doing that.

"I would like some time to think about this." Karis said after a brief silence.

"I agree," Breanna said. "This is not something to rush into. I need some time with it too - to be comfortable with the idea that this is our only option."

"I would expect no less," Conley stated. "You both understand that it is a time-sensitive issue, that the sooner we make a decision the better, but I have had time to think it through. Would twenty-four hours be enough?" At their nods he continued. "Fine then, let's meet here tomorrow night, say around 9 p.m.?"

With that they all stood and stowed their confidential papers in the secure files located against the back wall of the room. They gathered their things, and, keeping with tradition, they all left The Secure Chambers together. The heavy weight of the decision before them silenced the idle chatter that usually followed one of their meetings. They all quietly said their good-byes and went their own ways, each of them distracted by his or her own private thoughts.

CHAPTER 10

Max

Max lay awake in his sleeping bag, letting the thoughts of Mara wash over him. He didn't do this often, but he was too tired to fight it tonight. Along with the deep sadness that always accompanied these memories, he felt a sense of peace. It had felt good to talk about her to their daughter. He knew that Anya hungered for information about her mother, and selfishly he had always put her off - it was just too painful. Finally Anya had stopped asking questions, and he would be lying to himself if that hadn't relieved him. Tonight, though, made him begin to wonder if he had been wrong all those years. It was as if, by talking about the good memories with Mara, the horror of what had happened in the end was pushed deeper, farther back in his mind. It became more of a stinging slap to the face and less of a sucker-punch to his gut.

Oh, he missed her terribly. It was always there. In all the years she had been gone, he'd never gotten over the loneliness for her. It wasn't just having someone there he missed - it was having Mara there. She'd always understood him like no one else, and she'd accepted his failings just as fully as she'd accepted his strengths. He'd lost track of the number of times he'd turned to say something to her, or the countless times his heart would skip a beat when he'd see a woman who resembled her in some small way. He had hoped that over the years that ache would eventually be replaced by numbness, but after 16 years he was still waiting.

He shifted in his sleeping bag and felt the familiar knot of pain begin to take root in his stomach, but this time, instead of willing it away with thoughts that were as far removed from Mara as he could get, he focused hard on happy memories of her.

Max took a deep breath and closed his eyes, trying to immerse himself in one of his favorite memories of her. The one that came to him immediately was the day that they found out Mara was pregnant. He had been so busy at the hospital that she hadn't wanted to mention that she'd been feeling "off" for some time. He laughed remembering how like her that was. She was not going to let anything stop her for long, especially not some silly stomach bug. So she drank orange juice like crazy, popped her daily vitamins, and started carrying a toothbrush with her for those times when lunch just wouldn't stay down. Her plan was the same as it had always been; she would fight through this flu and not budge an inch - not even acknowledging it to herself, let alone her husband. But, when several weeks went by without the symptoms subsiding, she thought it might be time to see someone.

Max smiled softly remembering the look of shock on her face as she walked into the emergency room that afternoon. Of course, he'd known nothing about her visit to the doctor that morning so he was totally unprepared to see her standing in front of him. The look on her face arrested him in mid-sentence. It was wonder, fear, shock, and joy all wrapped into one. He didn't know what had brought her there, but he knew from that moment their lives would be different.

He didn't remember walking over to her, but suddenly he found himself standing before her. "Mara? What are you doing here? Is everything okay?"

She looked at him in dazed wonder and said,

"I...Could we?" She paused. "Is there someplace we could talk?" she finally ended, taking notice of the curious stares they were beginning to elicit.

He didn't care about anybody else, he just knew they were not moving from that spot until she told him what was going on. "What's wrong?" he asked. "Just tell me what's going on."

She could hear the note of panic that was beginning to creep into his voice and knew him well enough to know that he was not going to budge. She gave in, smiling a soft smile and quietly whispered, "I just came from the doctor." At his look of fear she quickly continued, "We....we're going to have a baby."

Time seemed to slow down. He'd heard the words, but it was if the message hadn't gotten to his brain. A baby. They were having a baby. Before he realized what he was doing, a loud "Woop!" escaped him as he scooped her into his arms. Finally, it was Mara's voice that got through to him.

"Max! Max! Maxwell!"

He stopped and realized they now had everyone's attention. Mara's cheeks were flushed with embarrassment. He quickly put her down and grabbed her hand, "Come on!"

"What? Where are we going?" she asked as Max dragged her past the nurses' station and down a hallway to their left.

He turned with a broad smile and a twinkle in his eye and would only say, "You'll see."

He led her to a long corridor lined with doors. It was obvious that these were private exam rooms. He did a quick survey of the lights above the doors that signified which rooms were occupied and found that the last door on the right was free. He opened the door and immediately began rifling through the drawers and cupboards.

"Will you tell me now what you are doing?" Mara asked. He wasn't fooled. He could hear how she had to force the impatience into her voice. Yep, it was all bluster.

"Hop up," he responded as he continued searching for what he wanted.

"Excuse me?"

This time he turned and smiled. "Hop up," he pointed to the exam table in the middle of the room. "Right there. Hop up and I'll be with you in a second." He turned back to searching and heard the impatient burst of air that escaped Mara. He smiled as he heard her mumbling something about him being ridiculous, but she got up on the table anyway.

"Ah ha! Here it is!" he exclaimed, as he pulled out a small walkie-talkie like machine with a small cylindrical device attached. He turned to Mara and said, "Now, lay back." At her dubious look he paused and softly said, "Trust me."

Mara rolled her eyes and did as he asked. He switched on the machine and rolled up her shirt to expose her stomach.

"Max, I really don't think -"

"Shhhh," he said, "listen." Max placed what Mara realized was a microphone to her stomach and searched for a few seconds. It seemed like they both held their breath as they listened to the silence, and then they heard it, the soft woosh, woosh, woosh, of a tiny heart beating. Max moved the microphone a few millimeters and it got a bit louder. He knew that the wonder he was feeling was mirrored on her face. He held it there a few minutes more and then reached for Mara.

Now, lying in his sleeping bag and looking up at the canvas of his tent, Max realized that the moment in that tiny exam room was what had made that day his favorite. For it was the day when he knowingly held his family in his arms for the first time, a family that was healthy and full of promise for a bright future, a family that was whole and without scars. He closed his eyes and felt his limbs grow heavy with exhaustion. His last thought before sleep overtook him was that the ball of tension had eased and was replaced by a languid peace. The time for the dark secrets would come later, but tonight he would hold on to the light.

***

Max came awake the next morning slowly, realizing it had been a long time since he'd slept that soundly. He lay there for a moment breathing in the fresh cool air of the morning and stretching as much as the small tent would allow for his lanky frame.

He heard Anya moving around in the camp. She was always up early, so this didn't surprise him in the least. He hoped the clanking that he was hearing also indicated she'd gotten a pot of coffee going. There weren't too many things he enjoyed more than his morning cup of coffee.

He unzipped his sleeping bag and reached for the sweatshirt that was folded in the corner of the tent. He always slept fully clothed, a lesson that had been drilled into him at The Center, but he knew how crisp the morning mountain air could be so he always left his sweatshirt within easy reach. As he pulled the soft cotton over his head, he froze, an instinctive reaction to the muffled voices he heard outside. When he recognized Anya's as one of the voices it took all he had not to go bursting out of the tent, but caution was also a lesson that he had learned well.

He finished pulling on his shirt and moved to quietly fasten his leather ankle scabbard, containing a sharp dagger, to his leg. He made sure it was well hidden beneath his loose pant leg before removing the hunting knife from beneath his pillow, which he then stowed in the specially-designed sheath at his waist. All the while he was listening closely to the sounds that were drifting in from the campsite. So far he only heard one other voice besides Anya's. It seemed to be coming from an older male who, if the amount of talking was any indication, had no need for stealth or secrecy. Max knew better though; many thieves traveled in packs and sent in a distraction to draw attention away from what was really happening.

Realizing that Anya was not in any immediate danger, Max crept slowly out the back of his tent and into the foliage of the woods. He would do a careful sweep of the surrounding area to make sure there would be no surprises. His tracking skills had always left something to be desired, according to Mara, but he had discovered that they were more than adequate for life beyond The Center.

As he carefully circled their campsite he came to a spot that drew his attention. It was a spot below a large pine tree about three yards from the perimeter of their site. There was nothing obvious, just a small clearing where there typically would not be, as if someone or something had bedded down for the night. He saw no signs of a human presence, but he had learned early on to trust his instincts, and something about this was not right.

He did a quick scan of the surrounding area and

then hunkered down to get a closer look. There were no shoe prints, in fact the area looked a bit too clean, as if someone had worked hard to cover their tracks. He turned and realized that from this vantage point there was an unobstructed view of their site. If someone were watching them, this would be the perfect place to be. Max figured if that was the case, whoever it was had moved on and would not be coming back to this spot.

He wondered briefly if their morning visitor had been here, watching them last night as they sat around the campfire talking, but that theory didn't feel right. Someone who took this much care hiding themselves would not boldly stroll into their campground; they would be more likely to hide in the shadows and strike when they were least expecting it.

He continued on, scanning the trees and the ground for other evidence but found none; it seemed that whoever had stumbled upon them had come alone. Before breaking through the trees to reveal himself, Max paused on the edge of the clearing and let his eyes go to work. His first discovery was that he had indeed been right about an older man doing all the talking. He was just as Max had imagined him, probably in his mid to late 60's with the deep lines and swarthy skin of a man who lived the hard life of a traveler. His clothes were baggy and worn, perfect for hiding weapons or small valuables that found their way into his sticky fingers. He had a leather knapsack that had seen better days at resting by his feet, and close enough to grab if a quick exit was needed. Max watched a bit longer as Anya moved to refill the man's coffee cup. The smile he offered her seemed genuine enough, but Max still had the feeling that this man was not what he appeared to be.

A movement to the left drew Max's attention away from the old man and it was then that he discovered the old man had a traveling companion. The boy was young -- maybe 17 or 18, on the cusp of manhood -- with jet-black hair and the olive completion that marked him as one of the Outlanders. If the old man oozed ease and charm, this boy was the exact opposite. He emitted a tension and a watchfulness that suggested he expected a threat at any moment. He did not say a word and seemed to be deep in his own thoughts, but Max knew better. This was a boy that missed no detail; Max knew he had already scoped out potential blind spots, and had deliberately chosen for himself the most strategic position that the site offered. It was his presence that told Max that these two had not simply stumbled upon them haplessly. This was a young man who knew where he was and what he was about at every moment. This meeting was no accident, of that he was now certain.

As Max exited through the trees, three sets of eyes looked in his direction. Anya's and the boy's held surprise, but it seemed that the old man was sharper than he had given him credit for. He'd known someone was watching them, and wasn't at all startled by Max's entrance.

"Um, Dad," Anya began hesitantly looking from where he had exited the woods to his tent across the clearing. Clearly she'd been unaware that he was not still fast asleep, as she'd expected. "Um...yeah, Dad this is Gus and his grandson, Koen." Max heard the nervousness in her voice and knew it was not because of the strangers, but because she was unsure as to his reaction to them in their camp.

He nodded to Gus and sent a similar nod of acknowledgement to Koen, but refrained from extending them a welcome beyond that. He continued in through the clearing and made his way behind Gus in order to position himself closer to Anya.

"They're heading north, to The Capital City," Anya said. Max could tell she was uncomfortable with the tension that filled the air, and that was just fine with him. She knew better than to let strangers into their camp, and even worse, to not alert him to their presence. They would be talking about this later - assuming there would be a later when they could.

He shot her a look that gave her no doubt as to what he was thinking, then said slowly and deliberately, "Is that so?"

"Yes sir!" Gus broke in. "We're heading to the city to find work."

"Indeed." Max responded. "What kind of work is it you are looking for, exactly?" The feeling that these two were not what they appeared to be did not leave Max, but he sensed no immediate threat from them. Even so, he was not going to lower his guard. He walked in front of Anya and took a seat across the cook fire from Gus. He made a small motion with his head, indicating that Anya was to remain in the background. He knew she had gotten his signal when she drifted off toward her tent and began organizing their fishing equipment.

"Well, we'd do just about anything that needs doin'," Gus responded, but his sharp green eyes belied the casualness of his words. "These are hard times, are they not?"

Max contemplated that last question and batted away the whisper of fear it caused. He had hoped the unease he'd been feeling for days was merely the dredging up of long buried ghosts from the past. Now he wasn't sure.

Gus lifted his mug and drained the remains of his coffee. "Well, we thank you for your kindness," he said as he stood, "but it's past time for us to be going."

Max and Koen stood as well, while Anya turned from what she was doing, keeping her distance from the men.

Gus raised the empty cup to her in a salute of thanks for the coffee, and then placed it on the ground. He'd gotten the message loud and clear that they were to maintain their distance from Anya, and he would respect that. He turned and took several slow steps toward his grandson, working out the stiffness from sitting as he went.

Even from across the camp Max saw the concern in Koen's eye as he watched his grandfather's slow progress. The old man would have a difficult time traveling the many rough miles it would take them to get to The Capital City.

"May your travels be safe and light," Max said, offering them the standard traveler's benediction, and meaning it sincerely.

Gus turned and acknowledged Max's words with a nod. After a slight hesitation he spoke, taking time to choose his next words carefully. "These woods are filling with many travelers, searching for all sorts of things." His eyes shifted to Anya briefly and then back to Max, glowing with intensity. "Keep her close," he said, soft enough for only Max to hear.

The sudden pit in Max's throat made it hard to swallow. He understood that Gus's words were meant in warning and not in threat - that this had been the purpose of their visit all along. They were there to make sure Max knew something was coming, and that it concerned Anya. The suspicion that he was in the presence of an actual Seer took root in his mind. He fought the desperate urge to call Gus back and ask for explanations - to beg him for further information. Instead, he nodded to Gus, knowing that he was given all that he would need - for now anyway.

Max watched the pair until they were out of sight, breathing deeply and constructing plans. Gus's warning would not go unheeded. He had learned long ago the folly of not listening to the warning of a Seer. He would not make the same mistake twice.

CHAPTER 11

Conley

"What is our status, Captain?" Conley tried hard to keep the impatience out of his voice, but he knew they were running out of time. They needed a replacement, and they needed one now.

Hawkins shifted uncomfortably in his seat, drawing Conley's gaze to the numerous medals and patches that adorned the man's uniform. Despite his being older and highly decorated, they both knew who was in control. Conley knew that Captain Hawkins disagreed with his plan, thinking that his scouts would find The Chosen in enough time. There was a reason that Conley had called this meeting where and when he did. He wanted to make it absolutely clear to Hawkins who was in charge.

"We have the candidates narrowed down to two," Hawkins replied after clearing his throat. "We are just finishing up the background checks and family histories."

"Is there one that stands out?"

"There is," Hawkins said as he reached for one of the files on his lap and handed it across the desk to Conley. "His name is Ranae. Ranae Mondry."

Conley opened the file and quickly scanned the papers before him. He could easily see why this young man would stand out. His marks were some of the highest Conley had ever seen, and unlike most Storm Children, Ranae showed proficiency in several talents. On paper he seemed to be the perfect candidate for what they were looking for, but Conley knew that paper only told part of the story. He would have to meet the young Mr. Mondry in person in order to know for sure.

"He's twenty," Conley said picking up the picture that had been provided in the file, "rather old to still be a trainee."

"He was a late admission," Hawkins said, answering Conley's implied question as to why someone that old was still at The Center. "He didn't begin his training until he was ten."

Conley raised his eyebrows in surprise. This was highly unusual. Typically, Storm Children came to The Center as infants, or at the very least as toddlers, but to begin at ten years old? That was something Conley had never heard of.

"Apparently he'd been in one of the city's orphanages when he was nine. It took a year for the staff to realize that he was a Storm Child and then send him to The Center." At Conley's nod, Hawkins continued, "There is very little information on him. No parents are listed on any of the paperwork we can find. All we know is that he'd been picked up by one of the patrols. He'd been living alone on the streets."

Conley looked down at the photo he was holding. The young man in the picture was not smiling like the majority of the Trainees did in their yearly pictures. Instead, there was a seriousness that bordered on a kind of hunger in his piercing blue gaze that merely added to his obvious charisma. His golden hair was closely cropped and only served to accentuate his classic handsomeness.

"He remembers nothing?" Conley asked.

"Very little, Counselor," Hawkins replied, "and only of his time living on the streets. He has no recollection of any time before that."

Conley considered what Hawkins just said and began to think that Mondry's lack of family and past could actually be an asset in this situation. It would certainly make the deception less complicated.

Conley's thoughts were interrupted by the buzz of the intercom. Mrs. Martyn knew he was not to be disturbed, so this had to be an emergency. Conley picked up the handset and listened to Mrs. Martyn's explanation.

"I'm sorry to interrupt, Sir, but it's the doctor, and he says it's urgent," Conley heard in his ear.

"Of course," he told her, "put him right through." He had felt this was coming, and had been dreading this conversation.

He was aware of Hawkins's intense interest in the call, but Conley ignored him, focusing all his attention on what the doctor was telling him.

Letting out a deep sigh he finally spoke, "Thank you, doctor. I appreciate the information. I'm sure it will go without saying, but considering the delicacy of the situation, I trust I can count on your complete discretion. We will begin making arrangements and let you know when we plan to make a statement." He waited a moment and then replaced the phone gently in its cradle.

Conley took a deep breath and looked across the desk at Hawkins. "Counselor Wilcox passed away." He could see the deep sadness in Hawkins's eyes at the announcement - sadness that mirrored his own deep grief. He paused a moment giving them both a moment to let the news sink in, and then rose to his feet, causing Hawkins to follow suit.

"It looks like our time for waiting is over. We will need to act within the next twenty-four hours." Conley walked around his desk as Hawkins gathered his things.

They both understood that action was needed now. "Get Mondry and meet me in The Council Chambers in two hours."

Hawkins paused, looking up at Conley in shock. "But Conley, don't you think it prudent that we find out more about his background before we make a final decision?"

"What I think is 'prudent', Hawkins, is that you follow my directions," Conley returned sharply. He knew Hawkins was taken aback at his harshness, for Conley always treated him as more of a confidant, and had never pulled rank before. He regretted his outburst immediately, but they didn't have time for second thoughts or background checks.

Hawkins's face flushed red and his back stiffened, "Of course, Counselor Fitzgerald," he replied. "Everything will be just as you have requested." He gave Conley a short nod and a rigid bow, then turning sharply, he quietly left the room.

Conley dropped his head and pinched the bridge of his nose, hoping to get some relief from the sudden tension headache that was threatening. Once this was all over, he would sit down with Hawkins and apologize, but right now he needed to get in touch with Karis and Breanna. They no longer had the luxury of time. They needed to reach a decision within the hour.

His head came up when he heard a knock on the door. Mrs. Martyn stood at the entrance to his office with her notebook firmly in hand, waiting for permission to enter, knowing without having to be asked that he would be needing her help. He nodded gently in appreciation and gestured her to take her normal seat while he walked back to his desk. He couldn't bring himself to sit just yet, so he turned to study the morning light shining on the city.

"First we must gather The Council." Here he paused briefly accepting that Leander would no longer be on her list to call. He took a deep breath and continued giving her directions, listening to the soothing scratching of her pen on paper.

CHAPTER 12

Anya

She'd been on pins and needles all afternoon, waiting for Father to start in on her about letting Gus and Koen into their camp. She understood why he would be mad; even now she wasn't exactly sure why she'd done it in the first place. It wasn't like her to trust strangers, but there was something about Gus that made her know she would be safe.

Koen was something different all together, though. He had immediately put her on edge, and she wasn't sure why. It certainly wasn't something he said, since he hadn't uttered a sound the whole time he was with them. It wasn't anything he did to her either, in fact, other than a quick glance when his grandfather introduced him, she could have been invisible. She'd noticed that he kept scanning the trees, as if he were expecting to see something. It had made her jittery and nervous, like she should be looking over her shoulder or something.

She heard her father sorting through the things in his tent. Was he going to give her the silent treatment all day? She could feel her own anger rising to the top. She understood; she wasn't supposed to talk to strangers, but was he going to hold it against her for the rest of her life? She'd just decided that enough was enough, when her father's loaded pack came flying out of his tent.

Before she could process what that could mean, her father crawled out and looked up at her. She'd expected anger, or at least disappointment, but when she saw the flash of fear she began to get nervous. Was he really that angry with her? Angry enough to cut their weekend short?

"Look Dad, I'm sorry," she began, "I know I shouldn't have invited them in, but -" She stopped talking, feeling miserable and not knowing what else to say.

Her father stood up and put his hands on her shoulders. "Listen, Anya I know you feel bad about this morning," he sighed, "but I understand."

Anya raised her eyes to his face, trying to read what he wasn't saying. He'd gotten control of his emotions and wasn't giving anything away, she knew something was there though; something was giving his words an intensity she didn't comprehend.

"I do," he said, giving her shoulders a comforting squeeze. At her wince he was momentarily distracted from their conversation. His eyes flew to her shoulder and what she saw then made her uneasy. He looked back at her and took a moment to search her face. What was he looking for?

And then - nothing. No questions about her shoulder, no nagging about taking it easy, no nothing. He dropped his hands and turned around to grab the pack at his feet. This was not like her father at all; he never let things like this go. What was going on? "We will be leaving at first light tomorrow," he said as he threw the pack closer to the side of her tent. "I suggest you take this time to get your things packed up and ready to go. We would be leaving now if I thought we had enough daylight to get home, but as it is we'll have to spend one more night here."

If he had turned around at that point he would have seen the devastation clearly written on her face, but he didn't.

"I'm going to gather enough firewood for tonight. I won't be long," here he paused and finally turned back to her. "Don't leave the camp, Anya - for anything. Do you understand?"

All she could manage was a stiff nod before he turned and left the clearing. She managed to make it into her tent before the first tears began to fall.

CHAPTER 13

Max

Max heard Anya moving around in her sleeping bag, trying to get comfortable, and he sighed. They'd shared a miserable evening and he was relieved when she'd announced that she was going to bed early, *since they were leaving so early,* was how she'd put it.

Max hadn't taken the bait; he'd just let her go with a quiet good night. He knew she had been upset earlier, and in his defense, he'd been about to explain to her that he wasn't angry, but then he'd squeezed her shoulder.

At her wince he'd had an immediate flashback of that morning in the bathroom with Conley, the day his Mark had appeared. He'd been so flooded with fear, standing there with Anya, that he'd had to leave. He couldn't let her see that, let alone tell her it was not anger that was driving him to leave, but fear.

He felt calmer now, sure that it was just all of the old memories he'd been dredging up, and the warning from Gus this morning that put him on edge, but he wasn't going to take any chances. He'd decided that he would keep watch tonight. He could get some sleep once they were home and Anya was safe.

The rustling had finally stopped in Anya's tent. He shifted on the hard ground, stretching his legs out in front of him, and adjusted the pack he'd been leaning against so he could sit more comfortably. He pulled his small blanket tighter around his shoulders in an effort to shut out the biting wind. It was going to be a long night. Hopefully Anya would be asleep now, and she would be able to get a full night's rest. It would be good if at least one of them did.

***

It was the screaming that pulled him sharply awake. He must have dozed off, and had no idea if what he'd heard had been reality or the echo of a long forgotten nightmare - until he heard it again.

Anya.

The only things he checked as he flew to her tent were that he had his knife and his flashlight in hand. Whoever, or whatever, was causing his daughter to scream in such agony would not be long for this world.

The site that greeted him when he entered took a moment to register to his sleep-drugged senses. Anya lay, alone, in her tent writhing in pain amongst her blankets. She wore only her tank top and shorts, but looked as though she had soaked those through with her own sweat. Her face was contorted in agony and long tendrils of her hair were clinging to her cheeks and neck.

Seeing no outside threat, Max kneeled at her side and ran the light up and down her form, trying to look for any small insect or animal that may have caused this reaction. Seeing nothing, he touched a hand to her forehead and discovered that she was burning with fever.

Max scanned the tent with the light and noticed her water bottle in the corner. He stood the flashlight on end and poured some of the cool water into his hands. He turned and bathed her face, hoping to offer her some relief from the heat.

"Dad?"

"Shhh, don't talk, Anya," Max soothed.

"It's burning," she got out.

"No, you've got a fever," Max told her. "I'll get you cooled down. It's just a fever," he repeated. He wasn't sure if he was now comforting himself or her.

"No," Anya said. "No Dad. It's burning. *It's* burning."

Now he was confused. "What? What's burning, Anya?" His eyes ran the length of her, looking for some wound or bite that would tell him what he needed to do to relieve the fire that was raging in her.

"Shoulder," she whispered through her parched lips, "shoulder on fire."

Max could taste the metallic tang of fear. This could not be. Not again. Not Anya.

Time seemed to slow as he saw his hand reaching out to turn her over. His mind was screaming at him not to do it, but his body would not obey. Slowly, gently, he shifted Anya to her left side, exposing her right shoulder.

At first he thought he saw nothing, and he began to breathe a sigh of relief, but then something changed. Wanting to make sure it wasn't just his eyes playing tricks on him, he reached back and grabbed his flashlight, shining it on Anya's shoulder.

That's when he saw it. There under the thin strap of her tank top were the painful welts of blistered flesh. Welts that were in a clear pattern, a pattern he had seen only once before in person. A pattern that was unmistakable. There was no doubt about it, what had begun as a whisper of dread, now became their reality. Anya had been chosen.

***

Far away, in a long forgotten place, an old man sat looking out a window. He heard the servant enter behind him, but he didn't bother turning around.

"Excuse me, Sir, but I just got the message," the man began. "It has begun. The plan is in place." The thin servant waited patiently after delivering his message, knowing that he was not to leave until he'd received his next instructions.

"Take care of the details," the old man instructed. "We leave for the City at dawn."

"Of course. As you wish, General." the man executed a small bow before he took his leave, despite the fact that his employer's gaze never wavered from the windows.

The old man heard the door close softly behind him and only then did he allow the satisfied smile to spread across his face.

CHAPTER 14

Anya

When Anya finally awoke she remained unmoving, afraid that the slightest motion would bring back the searing pain from the night before. She could still feel a tingling, a slight burning in her shoulder, but it was nothing compared to the heat and agony of the night. She mentally took stock of her body and her surroundings. She was still bundled tightly in her sleeping bag, and she could feel the slight pressure of the bandage her father must have wrapped around her wound. She took a deep breath and could tell by the smell of dew that the day was fresh - approaching dawn. The quiet of the morning finally gave her time to think. *What had happened last night?*

She remembered the fight with her father and the tears that followed. She remembered lying awake until she heard him come back from gathering wood. She remembered holding her breath as he paused outside her tent and let out a sigh that told her he regretted his harsh words. She remembered slowly letting out her own breath as he moved back to his own tent and settled in for the night. At some point she must have fallen asleep, because her next memory was of a pain like no other. She'd felt as if she were on fire. She must have cried out, because almost instantly her father was there, asking her what was going on. At first she was so overcome with the pain that she couldn't even locate its source, but somehow her brain finally registered that her shoulder was the source. She was able to get the words out to let him know that's what hurt, and vaguely she could recall him gently turning her for a better look, but after that, everything went blank. She must have passed out.

She heard a slight rustling to her right and dared a slow turn of her head. Lying beside her was her father. She took stock of his features, noting the clear exhaustion etched there. It was as if he'd aged ten years in one night. She must have made some sort of noise, because his eyes suddenly popped open and ran over her features, looking for any sign of lingering pain. He must not have seen any because he allowed himself a slight smile.

"Hey there, Kiddo. How are you feeling?"

He hadn't called her "Kiddo" since she was about eight. She could tell he was trying hard to keep his voice steady and calm, but she saw the worry in his eyes as clear as day, along with something else. Was it fear? What could possibly have put that spark of terror in his eyes? Was she that bad off? Was she dying?

She took a steadying breath to calm her own alarm, but it still crept into her voice. "It doesn't hurt as much. What was it? What is wrong with me?" She had to clamp her teeth together on her last words; otherwise the panic might take over.

"Here," he said, as he reached for her to gently turn her onto her left side. "Let me take a look under the bandage." She couldn't help but notice that he'd avoided her question, but she became momentarily distracted by the ache of shifting her body.

"I couldn't see quite as clearly as I would have liked last night," her dad continued as he gently helped her to shift and gingerly raised her arm in order to remove the bandage he'd put on. "I put some salve on it before I bandaged it up, but I wish I had the kind that really deadened the pain."

"What is it? Why is my shoulder on fire?" She couldn't keep the panic out of her voice this time, and she felt his fingers momentarily still.

"Let me take another look at it, Anya," he said slowly, "now that I can see a bit better. Whatever it is, you are not in any immediate danger." Did that mean this was something that would affect her later? That at some point she *would* be in danger? She wished she could turn to discern the truth in his eyes, but right now that was impossible.

As he peeled the bandage away from her shoulder she expected the pain to increase, but miraculously the fresh air made it feel better. She let out a soft sigh as the cool air touched her shoulder. She gave it an experimental roll and said, "Well, whatever you did, it worked. The burning is totally gone, and the ache that's been there for days is almost gone too," she continued with another, bigger roll of her shoulder.

She'd expected some response from her father at that, but when he continued to be silent, she turned back to look at him. "Dad? Is anything still there?" She lifted her left hand to feel the spot that had burned so badly in the night, but her father stopped her movement.

"No!" he said sharply as he stopped her. Her surprise at his tone must have shown clearly on her face, because he gentled his voice when he continued, "It's still raw, we need to keep it clean and bandaged."

"But the air feels good. I don't see -"

"No!" The sharpness again had her eyes widening, but he quickly cleared his throat and tried again. "No, trust me. We need to get moving; the danger of infection is just too great while we hike back home. We will keep it covered today," he finished in his don't-argue-with-me tone and set to getting a fresh bandage on her shoulder.

She tried to get a good look at his face, to see what was in his eyes, but he wouldn't look up at her, and that was worrisome. There was something that was seriously bothering him, and she needed to know what that was, but there was also something whispering to her to leave it be...for now.

Once he was finished wrapping her shoulder snugly, he instructed her to get dressed; they would be heading out within the next twenty minutes. "And make sure that you wear something that will cover that bandage," he said, "I don't want the whole wilderness to know that I'm traveling with a lame duck." He tried to smile at his teasing, but it never reached his eyes, and that worried her. He left her tent, and she sighed as she gathered her clothes and stowed her gear.

Usually breaking camp was a fun and drawn-out affair, but she couldn't help but notice her father's urgency as they broke everything down. He wanted to get away from here, and he wanted to do it quickly.

It was while she was picking up a lone cup by the campfire that she noticed a strap at the end of the log where Gus had sat so comfortably yesterday. She reached for it and saw the leather satchel that he'd carried into camp. "Hey, Dad!" she said as she lifted it up and turned. "It looks like Gus..."

Her voice drifted off as she noticed how still her father was standing. When she'd called him, he hadn't turned to look at her but kept is gaze focused on a spot to the right, just outside the circle of their camp. When she turned, she hitched in a small gasp.

Standing just outside the tree line, between her

and her father, was a tall man. He looked big and muscular, but she couldn't tell for sure because of the large black oilcloth coat he wore. He had black hair that fell to brush his shoulders and served to partly obscure his face. His skin looked weathered and leathery, as if he spent much of his time outdoors. It wasn't his outward appearance, though, that immediately put Anya on guard; it was the way he was standing and the look in his black eyes. She knew he was trying to appear casual, as if he'd just happened by, but everything about him screamed tension and readiness. The man was lethal, and both she and her father knew that.

The man's eyes darted from her to her father, and Anya could see the moment he decided to give up any pretense as to why he was there. His eyes settled on her father when he finally said, "We don't have to do this. I'm just here for her."

Her father didn't say a word in response, and although he didn't move a muscle, he seemed to grow bigger and more menacing at the stranger's words.

At first she was confused as to what was happening, but then the calm that often overtook her when she was hunting settled on her shoulders like a familiar coat. She watched her father rock to the balls of his feet and prepare for battle. The stranger was focused on him as the immediate threat, but she knew that the minute she made a move he would be on her before she could blink. She started running through her options, strategizing what would be her best move, but then she looked at how tightly controlled her father was, and realized that the best thing she could do for him in this moment was to wait. She understood that the only person she would distract was her father, and she didn't want to do anything that might throw off his focus.

She wasn't sure what drew her attention, but for some reason her eyes flicked briefly to the bushes behind where the stranger stood. Something was off, something was not right. There. There it was. She narrowed her eyes and then saw clearly that there was someone crouched low, not moving, someone waiting for a chance to strike. She pushed down the panic that threatened to crawl up her throat. There were more of them. How many more were surrounding the camp? Her eyes darted around the trees looking for the others. They wouldn't stand a chance against a whole band of thieves. Not seeing any other anomalies, her silver gaze flashed back to the spot where she'd seen the other figure.

Without making a sound, the figure had moved and was now more visible to her. His golden gaze locked on her sliver one, and she caught the imperceptible shake of his head.

Koen.

Whether they had doubled back in order to get the pack that she still held in her grasp, or if Koen and his grandfather had never left to begin with, she wasn't sure, but that one motion told her they weren't alone. She had the brief thought that maybe they were working *with* the stranger, and Koen must have seen the uncertainty in her eyes, because the second shake of his head was slower and more deliberate. She understood he was there to help, that her instincts about them had not been wrong. She gave him the barest of nods in response.

She turned her attention back to her father and the stranger. It seemed that they had been frozen in that waiting stance for hours, but she knew it had only been seconds since the stranger had spoken. Her eyes didn't waver from the black gaze that was trained so intently on her father. If she hadn't been so focused, she never would have seen the subtle change that happened in them - right before he charged her father, with murder in his eyes.

CHAPTER 15

Conley

Ranae Mondry was even more impressive in person than on paper. Conley had made the decision that the initial meeting would take place in his office. As sensitive as this issue was, he would not break with the tradition that no one but The Council met in the Secure Chamber. He had gotten the reluctant approval of the remaining council members and was now going forth with his plan.

He would have liked to have had more time to get to know the character of Mondry, but there was only so much longer that he could keep news like Leander's passing a secret. Once again his inner voice questioned the wisdom of the plan he'd constructed. It reminded him that he had yet to pass the point of no return, but with no news from Hawkins's scouts, they had run out of options - they needed a fourth Council member, and they needed one now.

Ranae Mondry stood at stiff attention in front of Conley's massive desk. He was wearing the snug but comfortable uniform that marked him as one of the Center's trainees. The uniform was designed specifically to allow the wearer a full range of motion while at the same time keeping the skin cool and dry during long training sessions. It was clear that Mondry had been summoned right as he was heading out for morning exercises, otherwise he would have dressed more formally.

The fact that he was in the office of a member of

The Council didn't seem to faze him. Mondry stood with a confidence that just needed a small nudge into arrogance. He had assumed an "at ease" stance when General Hawkins had ushered him in, and he waited in silence for what was to come. Conley guessed it was his years on the street that gave him the patience to wait for someone else to make the first move. Conley had no illusions, though, that Mondry was idly waiting for him to tell him why he was there. He could see the intelligence in Mondry's blue gaze and knew that his measure had been taken, and his surroundings had been catalogued.

Conley was certain that Mondry was mentally and physically fit for what they were about to ask of him, but was he *good* enough? Was his heart honorable enough for the task ahead, and the aftermath that may follow? These were the only questions that gave Conley pause, the only questions to which he did not have a definitive answer. He gave a short nod to Hawkins, who was standing next to the young man, letting him know it was time to get things rolling.

"Welcome, Trainee Mondry," Conley said, as he walked around his desk and indicated the small seating area to the left. "Please join us." Conley motioned for Mondry to take the small couch while he and Hawkins each settled themselves into a high-back chair across from it. As Mondry sat, Conley noticed there was no hesitation or awkwardness in his movements. The more he observed, the more he came to the conclusion that Mondry was the only one for the job.

"I would have liked a bit more time to exchange pleasantries, but I'm afraid that is one luxury we don't have," Conley began. Mondry's blue gaze locked onto his and probed for answers as he continued, "I am sorry to say that I will need some assurances from you before we proceed."

Conley watched Mondry look between himself and Hawkins before he gave a small nod for him to continue.

"The nature of our discussion is one that will require an Oath of Secrecy from you." After a short pause Conley continued, "If you cannot give, and *keep,* such an oath, now would be the time to tell us, because once it is given, any breaking of the oath would be considered treason. And your extensive studies have certainly given you an idea of what we do with traitors, haven't they?"

CHAPTER 16

Max

In the seconds before the stranger rushed him, Max realized why he seemed familiar. This was the newcomer who had spoken to him in town, after Collins had been thumped in the head by that horse. It was this man's targeted probing, coupled with Anya's news of the peddler's gossip, that had prompted their camping trip to begin with. Yes, it was now clear to Max what he'd suspected from the beginning - the man was a scout, and he had come for Anya.

Max pushed back the fear of a father that threatened to over-take him and drew upon the training that had been drilled into him years before. The man was certainly larger than he was, but that didn't automatically give him the advantage. Max was quick, and he knew how to use the element of surprise.

The man rushed him; at the last second Max dropped to the ground and rolled to the left. He used the momentum that he'd gained to regain his footing while reaching for the knife he kept at his back. By the time he'd righted himself, he saw that he wasn't the only one that was now armed.

The stranger had pulled his own wicked knife, presumably from somewhere inside that long coat of his. The two of them were now circling each other, like a pair of dogs, waiting for the other to make a move.

"Come now," the man said, "no one needs to get hurt. All I want is the girl." When Max didn't respond, he continued, "My employer will be very interested to see her, *and* hear what I've found out."

This gave Max pause. His *employer*? That didn't

sound like he wanted to take her to The Capital and The Council. Could he have guessed wrong? Was the man not a scout after all?

"I hear when it appears, it burns terribly," the man said next, "as if a person is being branded from the inside out." He drew that last part out, seeing the flicker of truth in Max's eyes. Max knew it would be useless to protest, it was apparent that he'd been close enough to the camp last night to hear Anya cry out. The triumph in his black eyes told Max that he knew Anya had been marked.

Max opened his senses and could feel the impatience and excitement rolling off the stranger. Max knew that all he had to do was wait for that impatience to dictate his opponent's next move.

It was when he was taking inventory of his adversary that a movement in the bushes momentarily distracted him. In the split second that it took for his eyes to register that there was another person hiding just out of sight, the stranger made his move. The man lunged forward, circling his knife arm in a downward arc, anticipating Max's move to the ground. At the last second Max was able to bring his legs up, using one of them to deflect the knife. Max felt the searing pain in his thigh, but worked through that to plant his feet firmly in the man's chest, while grabbing the tails of his coat. Using all his strength, he pushed and sent the man flying over his head, causing him to land on his back. Max knew he only had a few seconds, while the stranger was trying to regain his lost breath, to secure the advantage.

As Max pulled himself upright, his hand landed on a large rock. Thinking fast, he grasped it and brought it down hard upon the stranger's head. Seeing that the man was no longer conscious, Max whirled around, looking for Anya and the other threat he'd seen in the bushes.

Anya remained standing where she'd been when the stranger had appeared; his brain registered that she was pale and her eyes were huge, but otherwise she was all right. It was then that he saw the tall, dark-haired figure next to her. He had his knife up and ready before his brain registered that it was Koen, and his posture was protective, not aggressive.

"Koen!" Gus yelled.

All eyes turned to the old man who walked from the woods, leaning heavily on his walking stick. "Get that man trussed up before he wakes up. Anya, get your father to sit down - before he falls down," he continued with absolute authority. This was not the feeble man who had walked out of their camp only yesterday; this man expected to be obeyed.

After a moment's pause, both young people jumped to follow his directions. Max felt Anya grab his arm and put it over her shoulders, while at the same time putting her arm about his waist.

"Dad?" Anya said, "Are...are you all right?" She paused as she helped him sit on a log. "Your leg...it's...it's bleeding."

At her words, the fire in his leg intensified, but he'd heard the worry in her voice so he took a moment to make his voice calm. "I'm all right," he said, "go get my pack, we need to stop the bleeding." When she hesitated, not wanting to leave him, he added a bit of sharpness to his tone, "Go, Anya!"

After a small startled jump, she was off. He watched Koen tying the stranger up tightly and divesting him of any hidden weapons. Max felt relieved that the man was still alive, and able to provide answers to the questions swirling around in his head.

Gus moved to his side, and after a heavy sigh, lowered himself onto the log next to Max. "So, Healer," he started, "how do *you* propose we get The Chosen to The Capital safely?"

Good question, thought Max. *A very good question, indeed.*

CHAPTER 17

Conley

"That will be all, Hawkins," Conley said in dismissal. He noticed Hawkins's brief hesitation before he nodded and slowly turned and left the room, closing the heavy wooden door softly behind him. Conley had needed him here to witness The Oath, and now that Mondry had given it, Hawkins was no longer needed.

"Please," Conley said as he once again indicated that Mondry should be seated. He reminded himself that what he was about to ask this young man was for the greater good, and then he began. "I'm sure that you have heard the news that Councilman Wilcox has been ill recently." Conley waited for Mondry to nod before he continued, "It was a bit more serious than the general public was lead to believe." He waited again, letting that sink in. "Last night he succumbed to the poison that he'd been given, and he passed away." Conley had deliberately mentioned poison, wanting to see his reaction. Other than a slight widening of his eyes, Mondry remained stoic and silent, waiting for Conley to continue. "The Mark has not appeared -"

"That you know of," Mondry broke in.

Conley's eyes flew to Mondry's, "Pardon?"

"That you know of, Sir," Mondry repeated. "The Mark has not appeared...as far as you know."

Conley paused; he should have known that this young man would have immediately understood their dilemma. "Yes," Conley sighed, "I see you understand our problem. If The Mark had shown up on one of the Trainees, we'd know about it, but such is not the case. It is now clear that we have no idea where The Chosen is."

"Scouts are looking?" Mondry asked.

Conley had to fight the urge to pinch the bridge of his nose, "Yes," he said as he stood and walked to the sideboard to pour himself a glass of water. He turned and raised his glass, asking silently if Mondry would like some as well. Mondry shook his head and Conley continued, " Scouts have been scouring The Outlands." He returned to his seat and placed his glass carefully beside him. "Nothing. They've found nothing, and now we've run out of time."

After a short pause Mondry asked, "And how do I factor in?"

"You are to become the newest member of The Council. You, my boy, are to be hailed as the next Chosen."

CHAPTER 18

Anya

It looked bad. The angry gash that split open his thigh had to hurt, but her father remained still as Anya bound the wound. It needed stitches, even her untrained eye knew that, and if they would have been home, her father would have gone straight to his office and gotten ready the needle and thread - but they weren't home. They were in the middle of nowhere, surrounded by strangers. From what the man who had attacked her father had said, he seemed to know about her shoulder, about what had happened the night before. He'd even described it perfectly, *like being branded from the inside out,* he'd said. How had he known? Anya wanted answers, but she needed to get her father taken care of first. She was certain that this was only the beginning, that there would be others looking for her. They needed to get moving, and fast.

Her father must have felt the panic that was threatening to overtake her, because he put his hand on hers, stopping her momentarily from wrapping his leg. "We have time, Anya," he said as she met his eyes, "Not much, but some before we have to move."

She took a deep breath and nodded, slowing her movements slightly. She noticed that he hadn't told her that everything would be all right. She recognized the fact that he wasn't sure about that, and despite the lack of reassurance, she felt better.

"That's good, for now, Anya," her father finally said. "Why don't you finish getting our stuff together?"

She knew a dismissal when she heard one. Anya looked back and forth between her father and Gus, and knew that they were anxious to discuss what would happen next. Her first instinct was to argue, to voice her protest at being left out of a discussion that centered on her future, but the look in her father's eyes stopped her.

As she gathered the supplies and took them back to her father's backpack, she saw Koen. His back was to her as he walked the perimeter, scanning the trees for any possible movement and incoming threat. As soon as he'd finished tying up the scout, he'd gone straight back into the woods, presumably looking for signs of others close by. He must not have seen anyone, because soon enough he was back at camp. Even after he came back, though, he continued to be on guard.

She was putting everything back in order when she realized that even though Koen made her uneasy for some reason, she felt safer with him here. Her eyes darted back to him. Maybe it was that he seemed so strong and solid - so capable. Anya knew there were only a few years separating them, but he wasn't at all like the obnoxious boys she'd gone to school with. She sensed he had their arrogance, but with Koen it fit, he wore it well and was driven by confidence, not competition. He must have felt her speculative gaze, because she saw his shoulders stiffen slightly just before he turned and caught her eye.

Anya swore she saw annoyance in his eyes before he could hide it. *Did she irritate him?* Anya mentally reviewed her actions when he'd been around. She couldn't recall anything that might have irritated him. They'd barely spoken. She felt her own irritation come to the surface and cause her eyes to narrow slightly. *Fine! You don't like me, and I don't like you,* she thought. She knew it was childish, but she couldn't help it. With a quick nod he broke eye contact and went back to scanning the woods for threats.

Anya zipped up the bag a bit more forcefully than necessary and then stood to carry it to where her bag rested.

"Anya," her father called, "come here, please." Something in his voice made her pause. She had the feeling she wasn't going to like the solution they'd come up with.

"You too, Koen," Gus added. "We are safe for now."

Anya glanced in his direction and her unease increased. She watched Koen pause slightly and then walk towards his grandfather. Anya followed and took a seat next to her father.

"Anya must get to The Capital City as swiftly as possible," Gus began. "She is not safe out in the open, as we saw this morning." Gus must have seen the protest that Anya was about to voice, because he looked right at her when he continued. "They will only send more, Anya," he said. She swallowed her protest, because deep down she knew he was right.

"The only safe place for you is in The Capital City," her father continued. "We need to get you there as quickly as possible." She waited, knowing they weren't finished.

"It is a week's journey by foot," Gus said. "You will need to keep hidden and stay away from villages."

"Wait," Anya broke in, "'You'? Don't you mean 'we'?"

She saw it in her father's eyes before he said a word. "I can't go fast enough, Anya. It isn't safe for you -"

"I don't care!" she broke in. The panic started to claw at her. "I'm not leaving you!"

"Anya," Max began, "you and Koen -"

"No!" She stood to emphasize her point. "I *will not*

leave you." She'd spoken the words slowly, both to calm herself and to get her point across. She'd never known a time when she was away from her father, and now, when she felt the most vulnerable and frightened, he was asking her to go on without him? She *wouldn't.* She *couldn't.*

"He needs medical attention," Gus began, but Anya didn't want to listen to reason.

"I can go with him," she said. "We can stay hidden, I'm good at hiding and waiting."

"Anya..." When her father used that reasonable tone, she knew there was no swaying him, but she didn't want to listen to reason.

"Tell them," she demanded as she turned to Koen. "Tell them we can't go running off to The Capital City on our own!"

She saw it, she saw it in his face that delivering her to The Capital City was the *last* thing he wanted to do, but seconds later the mask of duty fell to cover it. "It is the only way."

With that she lost her last possible ally. Her eyes darted from Koen to her father, to Gus, and back to her father. She read it easily in their faces, the decision had been made and nothing, *nothing* she could say would sway them. She would be spending the next week with someone who, for some unknown reason, despised her, heading toward a place that she and her father had been running from her whole life. And as if that weren't enough, she'd be doing it all alone. She had never felt so miserable.

CHAPTER 19

Conley

For the first time Conley could remember, he didn't follow protocol when he got home that night. He'd dismissed his guard and dropped his briefcase in the foyer, instead of placing it carefully in the safe. It was a small act of defiance, but he was so tired of following the rules.

He let out a cynical laugh when he thought that. It seemed that he'd been doing a lot of rule-breaking lately. He'd broken the ultimate rule - the one that no one had broken in hundreds of years. *He'd* chosen one of The Council. In essence, he'd become a traitor to his people.

He realized that they had not reached the point of no return, only those in the inner circle knew of Leander's death, and the hole he'd left in The Council. It would only take a couple of calls, and the plan could be stopped, but he'd still had no word from the scouts that he'd sent to The Outlands. The Mark had to have appeared by now, so why hadn't they heard anything? No, they wouldn't be able to keep Leander's death a secret much longer, and then people would be clamoring to know who would take his place. If they didn't present The Chosen, Conley knew that a whole crop of fakes would suddenly rise up to claim their "right" to the position. To his way of thinking, it was better to have a fake you knew, than a fake you didn't.

He bypassed the kitchen and went straight back to his bedroom, seeking the bathroom beyond. He needed a shower and some sleep. Tonight he might even use those sleeping pills the doctors had given him some time ago. He suspected that without them it would be another sleepless night, and now that the ball was rolling, he needed all the rest he could get for the days to come.

CHAPTER 20

Anya

He wasn't human. She was absolutely convinced that Koen was at least eighty-five percent machine. They had been walking for hours, she had lost track how many hours a ways back. Now she was just concentrating on putting one foot in front of the other. There was no way she was going to ask to take a break or show any sort of weakness to him. She would keep walking until her feet broke right off, and from the way they were feeling, that should be any moment now.

Despite the fact that she'd put forth some good arguments about staying together, none of the men would be swayed. Finally, after watching the toll it was taking on her father, she relented. She would do as her father wished and go with Koen to The Capital City.

She still didn't understand why she couldn't take transportation from village to village like her father and Gus were planning to do, but for some reason they all seemed to think there was no way she was going to blend in. After what the scout who had come into their camp had said, they wanted to keep her safe, which meant away from as many people as possible. She'd also overheard her father say something about "check points", which made them all the more adamant about Anya staying away from civilization.

So, here she was, tromping through the woods with a machine-man, who apparently needed no rest or refueling. What she wouldn't give to be back at their hillside home, snuggled under her blankets, and listening to her father snoring softly in the next room.

Suddenly, she hit a wall that sent her falling

backward and landing in the dirt. She must have looked like a turtle lying there stunned and trying to get her bearings. Before she could spend too much time wondering what she'd run into, she looked up and saw Koen staring down at her. Apparently she'd been so deep in thought, or so exhausted from the day, that she hadn't noticed that he'd stopped walking, and rammed right into him. The fact that she actually felt like she'd hit a wall, was further confirmation of her machine-man theory.

"No, don't worry," Anya said, as she rolled over onto her knees so she could heft herself and her pack off the ground, "I'm just fine. I can get up on my own." She made sure to put an extra dash of sarcasm in that last bit, but suspected that it wouldn't "compute" anyway.

As she looked up to find a tree to grab onto, she suddenly felt her load lighten and the straps of her pack pull her up. Apparently Koen had decided to help after all, and hauled her upright by her pack alone.

"We'll stop here for the night," he said. "You stay here while I go gather some firewood."

Not even waiting for a response, he dropped his own pack and turned to go. Anya figured that arguing would take energy she didn't have, so she unhooked her own pack and set about making a bed for herself.

By the time he got back, she'd cleared a spot for a campfire and unpacked only the essentials she would need for the night. All her senses told her to be prepared in case they needed to leave quickly. As Koen began to organize the wood, Anya put together a simple meal. They would need to eat lightly for the next few days, until they reached the capital.

"Are you sure it's safe for a fire?" Anya hadn't

meant to speak her thoughts aloud, but the familiar task of setting up camp had lowered her guard and the question came out of its own accord.

"Yes." At first Anya thought that was all the answer she was going to get, but then he continued. "We are still far enough out that a small fire would not be seen. As we get closer, though, we will have to do without."

Anya paused in what she was doing to watch Koen in the fading sunlight. She saw how he'd deftly stacked the wood and expertly coaxed the flames into existence. He knew what he was doing. There was no hesitation, no uncertainty, in any of his movements. He seemed so certain - so capable. She thought back on their day and realized that from the moment they'd left her father she'd felt no fear. Oh, there were plenty of other emotions, but fear was not one of them. Koen may drive her crazy, but she felt safe with him, and after the day she'd had, that was saying a lot.

She sighed and walked over to where he was sitting. "Here," she said as she offered him some of the food she'd found. "It isn't much, but we need to ration what we have." She saw him hesitate, but then he reached for the food. His dark eyes reflected the firelight as they briefly settled on her face.

"Thank you," he said.

She sighed again and wearily headed back to where she'd left her blankets.

"Does it hurt?" she heard him ask.

"Excuse me?" she said. At the question she'd turned back to face him and had immediately stiffened. "Does what hurt?"

He seemed to hesitate again, almost as if he wished he'd never asked the question. "Your shoulder. You've been favoring it throughout the day."

Honestly, Anya didn't have any clue how to

answer. Koen knew what was there, but it was almost as if acknowledging it made it more real. She didn't want any of this, and if she ignored it, maybe it wouldn't be real. "I'm fine."

"I'm sure you are, but if you don't take care of that shoulder you may not be," was his quiet response.

"What's that supposed to mean?" Anya snapped.

"I heard your father tell you to keep your shoulder clean and to change the dressing each night. The last thing we need is for you to get some sort of infection." She could hear the tension in his voice.

"I will take care of it," Anya said as she turned back around and began walking away.

"Anya,"

Hearing him use her name for the first time made her stop in her tracks. She heard him sigh as he continued.

"Look, I know you don't want my help, but you need someone to look at it and apply the salve your father gave you."

She didn't move because if she did, she might break into a million pieces. She wanted to rage and cry at the same time, but she knew that she could do neither. Instead, she remained frozen and began taking deep breaths. She focused on the things around her in order to take her mind off the storm brewing inside. It was almost as if Koen knew she was fighting desperately for control, because he waited patiently, not saying a word.

After what seemed like an eternity, Anya whispered, "I will get the bandages."

CHAPTER 21

Koen

Koen let out the breath he'd been holding. He honestly had no idea if she would continue to fight him or if she would give in. He was relieved that her logic had won. It needed to be done and there was no one else to see to it. He watched her gather the supplies and reflected on their day. He knew that she'd been angry most of the day. He was glad because that anger discouraged conversation and had kept her going even when she was completely spent. They needed to cover as much ground as possible each day, and if that meant she had to be mad at him in order to do it, that was fine with him.

He was brought out of his thoughts when she suddenly plopped down in front of him. She didn't say a word, just handed him the bandages and salve and then presented her back to him. Slowly she unbuttoned her shirt and slipped her right arm out of the sleeve. He fished his small flashlight out of his pocket so he could better see what lay under her bandage. He waited a moment to see if she wanted to take the bandage off herself, but when she remained still he decided it was up to him. He placed the flashlight between his teeth and began to slowly remove the dressing. He felt a strange mixture of nervousness and curiosity. The mark she now carried was proof of the ancient stories that had been passed down for generations, stories he had always considered fanciful myth. He was about to view the proof that those tales were absolute truth.

"This is probably going to hurt," he warned her. He saw her slight nod and he took that to mean he was just to get the job done quickly. So he peeled back the bandage as quickly and as delicately as he could.

He hadn't realized that he was holding his breath until it came out in one big puff of air. There it was, the symbol of The Chosen, except it didn't look like the symbol that he'd seen so many times in his grandfather's books. That symbol was flat and lifeless, just some lines and a circle. This symbol seemed alive somehow. The pattern was dark and yet vibrant, in stark contrast to the white skin that served as its background. He also found it interesting that the symbol was raised and not flush with her skin. He could feel the heat radiating from her shoulder; it had to feel as if it were on fire. That made him realize that he had been staring a bit too long.

He cleared his throat and reached for the salve. "This should cool that shoulder down." He put some salve on his fingertips, but was hesitant to touch her. Would his rough fingers irritate her skin further? "Let me know if this hurts."

"Just get it over with," was all she said.

"Right," he said with a nod and then proceeded to slather her shoulder with the medicine. At one point he heard her sigh and realized that the salve probably felt refreshingly cool to her angry skin. He quickly placed a new bandage and then packed up the supplies as she straightened her shirt.

"Thank you," she said as he handed everything back to her. He gave her a quick nod in response. He had to admit he was a bit in awe of her. She was being forced down a path that he suspected she wanted no part of, and she was holding it together remarkably well.

He watched her, out of the corner or his eye, settle her blanket and lie down with her back to the small fire. After a few minutes he got up to stretch his legs. He would take another walk around the perimeter of the camp. He was sure there was no one following them, but he needed the distraction from his thoughts. He could tell from her breathing that Anya was out, so he felt safe grabbing his blanket and covering her with it before he left. It was doubtful he would be getting any sleep tonight anyway.

CHAPTER 22

Conley

It was amazing what a good night's sleep could do. In the bright light of day things didn't look so dire, in fact, Conley was certain that they would be able to pull this off. He'd spent the morning with Mondry composing the story of how his mark would appear and constructing a timeline of events. By this time tomorrow the city would be abuzz with the rumor that the new Chosen had been found. In two days' time they would officially announce the death of Leander and the identity of the new council member. Conley knew that both Karis and Breanna were holding out hope that they would still find the real Chosen, but Conley knew if The Chosen wanted to be found, it would have happened by now. He wasn't sure why The Chosen was remaining hidden, but he was positive that it was deliberate.

"And what happens to me when the real Chosen does appear?" Mondry had asked at their initial meeting. Conley had anticipated that question. He assured Mondry that *if* The Chosen was found, he would be well taken care of and that despite being branded a fraud and a fake, he would live out his days in peace and prosperity. He would be resigned to life in The Outlands, but he would want for nothing. It was a pretty good bargain for an orphan who was accustomed to very little. In the end, Mondry had agreed to the plan. Conley didn't tell him that even though he would publicly be a member of The Council, when it came to closed-door sessions and policy decisions, Mondry would be left out. After all, this was for the people's benefit; everyone on the inside was well aware of the pretense.

Conley reached over to the intercom on his desk, "Mrs. Martyn? It's time." He settled himself deeper into his leather chair. He knew she would be in momentarily with her trusty notebook and pen. They had a eulogy to write.

CHAPTER 23

Anya

Most mornings waking came slowly to Anya. It wasn't that she was lazy, or hated getting out of bed for that matter, it was more like her senses needed time to process all that was around her -- the feel of the bed beneath her, the temperature of the air around her, the sounds of the woods outside her window. Each of these things took time to come into her awareness each morning. Today, though, her waking was more like a rush of sensations, as if they were all dumped on her at once. Before she knew it she was sitting up and gasping for breath. She knew instantly where she was and what had transpired in the last 48 hours.

Her head whipped around, looking for Koen. She found him calmly erasing traces of their presence, completely ignoring her in the process. She looked down and saw the unfamiliar blanket that Koen must have put on her at some point. This kindness drew her eyes back to his face. He wasn't handsome in the traditional sense, his features were too harsh for that, but there was something about him that drew her in. He had the air of someone who was used to keeping secrets, someone who needed to be constantly on guard. She recognized that well, because she knew that she had an invisible barrier of her own. Maybe that was the connection she felt; she'd finally met someone who was a bit like her. No matter what village she and her father had ever lived in, she always knew there was something different about her. The other children had a confidence that comes when your family has lived somewhere for generations. She had never belonged.

"We need to get moving." Koen's voice brought her back from her musings. She realized that she had been staring at him for far too long. She gave herself a small shake and turned her head before he could see the embarrassed flush creep into her cheeks. She quickly folded the blanket and packed up the remainder of her things.

"There's a stream just that way if you want to wash up before we go," Koen said after a few moments. When Anya looked up, he was pointing to his right.

"Oh, right," she replied. "I'll just be a minute." She grabbed his blanket, and, as she passed by him, she dropped it on his pack and paused slightly. "Um, thank you for the extra blanket." She could tell that he was just as uncomfortable as she was, so she was thankful that his curt nod was the only acknowledgement that he'd heard her. She spun quickly around and headed off to get ready for another day of endless walking.

CHAPTER 24

Max

The same rocking that had finally lulled Max to sleep is what eventually pulled him from his dreams, that and the searing pain in his leg. After watching Anya and Koen leave camp, Gus had helped him do a better job of patching up his gash. From here on out he would make sure to have much more sympathy for those that he was stitching up. He was thankful that Gus had a good supply of alcohol to share. It wasn't pretty, and there was still the possibility of infection, but it would have to do. Max was currently sprawled in the back of a wagon, which was lumbering across the plains that marked the boundary between The Outlands and the villages that surrounded The Capital City. If he had had the energy he would have tried to prop himself up to see over the edge of the wagon, but he didn't. Instead, his mind wandered to the past twenty-four hours. Had it only been a day since his world imploded?

Once he'd taken care of his wound, the question became what should they do with the scout that was still out cold. Gus had picked through every pocket in that enormous coat, but as Max had suspected, there was nothing that would identify the man. Max recalled what the man had said before he'd been knocked out. He had mentioned an employer. That was one of the major pieces of the puzzle that Max didn't understand.

Max knew how new members of The Council were chosen. He remembered that Conley's mark hadn't shown up until one of The Council members was actually dead. The fact that Anya's was clear and visible was a good indication that they were one person shy of a full Council. It wasn't a stretch to imagine that if The Chosen hadn't presented themselves in The Capital City, they would be desperate to find them, and to find them quietly, lest they have a whole host of fakes on their hands. What bothered Max was the way the scout had tracked them and sought to take him out to get to Anya. He understood that to some of these scouts Anya was now a valuable commodity; she could be ransomed for a healthy haul, but there was something different about this one. Max kept coming back to that word *employer*. He kept gnawing on that one word in the hopes that a clue might finally present itself, but it had yet to reveal anything.

Gus, being a Seer, might be able to get something from the scout, but he couldn't do anything while he was out cold. They needed him awake to get some answers. Max had become concerned with the amount of time it was taking him to wake up. He knew it didn't take much of a blow to render a man useless, if you hit the right spot. He began to wonder if that's exactly what he'd done. It was while he was examining the head wound that a splash of water flew past his shoulder and hit the scout square in the face. Max had turned to Gus in surprise.

"We don't have time for this," was Gus's only explanation. It worked because the scout came awake sputtering and cursing. Max suspected this was not the first time this man was so rudely awoken.

"What the..." he began, and then abruptly stopped. Max watched as the memory of what had happened at the camp returned to the scout. If he hadn't been watching so closely, he wouldn't have seen the subtle shift in the scout's eyes. It was as if a shutter had been lowered over the secrets he held. "You won't get anything out of me," he said. "You should have killed me."

Max tried to open his senses, hoping to find any emotion that might be useful, but there was nothing, or what he thought was nothing. As he tried again he realized that there was a cover, almost like white noise, clouding any emotions that the scout was feeling. This was new to Max. Even at The Center he was able to feel *something* each time his trainers tried to block him. He looked back at the scout in surprise and watched as a slow smile spread across his face. Max realized he knew exactly what was going on.

Gus interrupted the moment, shoving Max out of the way and saying, "Move over. It's my turn now." Gus carefully placed his hands around the scout's head, making sure to align his palms with the scout's temples. Max watched Gus's thumbs press into his forehead as he closed his eyes.

Max could tell by the bead of sweat at the scout's hairline that he was using everything he had to counter what Gus was doing. Both men were pushing against each other, using enormous effort for the invisible battle they were waging. Gus's whispers became louder mumbles as he strove to hold on a bit longer, but soon enough his strength gave out and he collapsed, breaking the connection.

Instinct took over and Max rushed to help Gus, but was brought up short by his command. "No! Don't touch me," Gus rasped out. Even though his eyes were still closed, Max nodded and moved back to where they'd had their campfire the night before and sat down to wait.

It wasn't long before he saw Gus gain his feet slowly and walk to where he was. Gus looked exhausted, and sat down heavily beside him.

"I didn't get much," Gus began, "he learned somewhere along the way to protect himself from those with unique talents, but there were flashes. Most of them were meaningless, a tavern here, a village there, all meant to hide what he didn't want me to see. I got a glimpse, though." Here Gus looked at Max. "It was a hand, a powerful hand with a unique signet ring."

"Did you recognize the symbol?" Max asked.

"It is at the edges of my mind," Gus replied. "I know I've seen that symbol before. If I had my library with me I know I could find it, but we are not so fortunate. I do know this," here Gus paused and looked directly at Max. "I know that symbol does not bring comfort, quite the opposite in fact; the hand bearing that ring will bring much death and destruction before it can be stopped."

The lump that lodged in Max's throat at Gus's words was still there hours later. He knew Anya was a part of this, but until he knew more, he couldn't guess what part she would play, and that was killing him.

They had left the scout tied to the tree and gone to the nearest town to alert the authorities that there was a thief trussed up in the woods. Seeing the gleeful look in the sheriff's eyes, Max didn't think the scout would have to wait long to feel the heavy hand of the local justice system.

From there they had purchased a wagon and an old nag from a local farmer. Max was certain the farmer had gotten the better part of that bargain, but they didn't have time to argue. Max had wanted to set out immediately, but Gus had talked him into getting supplies and meeting with the local healer. His mind knew that was the right thing to do, but his heart pushed him to get back to Anya as quickly as he could. He understood that he wouldn't truly rest until he saw her again.

CHAPTER 25

Conley

Preparations were well underway. The people knew that something big was going on, after all, it wasn't every day that a large stage was constructed in the town square. In the Council Complex it seemed that everyone suddenly moved three times faster than the day before. Mrs. Martyn was in her list-making glory.

Conley took a moment to sit back in his chair and reflect on their last Council meeting. Karis had raised an important question. How would they fake The Mark? Each of them had gone through their own revelation ceremony, so they knew that Mondry's pristine back was an issue.

"Are you planning to brand the boy, Conley?" Karis had thrown out.

Conley knew she was trying to goad him by being so blunt. "You know that won't work," he'd calmly replied. Horrifyingly enough, others had tried this in the past. He still shuttered at the thought of parents branding their own children, just for the chance for them to be in a position of power. "Without going into needless detail, I will just tell you that I've used my own mark as a template for a prosthetic one Mondry will wear. No one will be close enough to examine it. I have every confidence that this will work for what we need."

"Of course you do," Karis had mumbled. Conley knew that he was meant to hear it, but he ignored the jab. He knew that both Karis and Breanna felt uneasy about this plan, and if he were honest with himself, he did too, but he saw no way around it.

A knock at the door interrupted his thoughts.

"Come in," he called.

Mrs. Martyn popped her head around the door, "Mr. Mondry to see you, Sir?"

"Yes, yes," Conley replied, reaching for the papers on his desk. "Send him in."

Once again, Conley was impressed with this young man's bearing. He walked with confidence and assuredness. To look at him, you would imagine that he would never question himself. He was just what the people of the city needed in a new leader.

"You wanted to see me, Sir," Mondry began.

"You know, you are going to have to get used to calling me 'Conley' or 'Councilman Fitzgerald' instead of 'Sir.'"

"Yes, Sir, but I believe we still have a few days until things are official," Mondry smoothly responded.

Conley sighed, "Yes, you are right. That is, in fact, why I wanted to see you. I wanted to walk you through the ceremony and see if you had any questions."

"I would appreciate that, Sir," Mondry said.

Conley paused. If he didn't know better, he would have guessed that Mondry was deliberately "sir-ring" him in order to irritate him, but his face was the picture of innocence. "All right then, have a seat and we can begin." Conley consulted his list and began going over the order of the ceremony, all the while pushing back the feeling of unease that kept tickling his senses.

CHAPTER 26

Anya

Anya had begun to lose track of time. Not only was she beginning to mix up sunrise and sunset, but she had to work to remember how many days they had been walking. They all had become the same and were now blurred into one long exhausting day. Yesterday the monotony had almost driven her mad, so she had started making up stories. This was something that she and her dad did often to pass time. They would make up the most entertaining stories about the people in the village. Her favorite one still was about how the baker's wife had once been an assassin for hire, which was quite hilarious considering how timid and frail she was.

To fight the weariness of the trail, Anya began making up stories about the animals she saw, but those got old quickly. After a while, she realized that she began to wonder about the young man who was walking so effortlessly in front of her. Soon her musings morphed into stories with Koen as the central character. Oh, they started out fantastical enough, with him being left on Gus's doorstep by a faerie creature who was seeking to hide the baby from an evil warlock, but this led to wondering about his actual past. She was so deep into her musings yesterday that she had mistakenly blurted out, "Where are your parents?"

The minute the words were out she knew it was a mistake. She held her breath, thinking that he might not have heard her, but she saw the hesitation in his step and knew that he had. She waited for a harsh word or a cold look, but nothing came. He'd just ignored her and continued on. Part of her was peeved beyond measure that he wouldn't even acknowledge her words, but the other part was hugely relieved that he hadn't. Since then she had made it a point to stay away from stories, especially ones that involved Koen.

Instead she did what she often did while hunting, she took stock of her surroundings and practiced strategizing. Instead of looking for animals, though, she began trying to find the best hiding spots and the best escape routes based on their position. Creating these "plans", as she called them, always made her feel energized. This time it was no different.

Before long, they reached a spot that would be perfect for their nightly camp. By now they'd fallen into a predictable rhythm and needed no words to get things settled. As Koen was out looking for wood, Anya inventoried their food. She realized with some surprise that this was now the fifth night they would be out by themselves.

"Tonight will be the last night we can safely have a fire," Koen said as he returned to camp and began stacking wood. "Tomorrow we will be getting close to the villages and therefore need to take extra precautions."

Anya's stomach jumped at his words. While it was just the two of them, she didn't have to think about what they were walking towards. "So, how long do you think it will be before we reach The Capital City?"

"Two days," was his short reply.

"What's the plan once we get there?" Anya asked, as she handed him the simple dinner she had prepared.

"Your father gave me a name," Koen replied. Anya waited, expecting more. When no more came, she lost her temper.

"That's it?" The harshness of her tone seemed to surprise him, because his head swiveled around to look at her. "That's all you are going to tell me? What is with all the secrets? Why can I never know the whole story?" Koen's eyes widened slightly as she continued to rant. "If my father would have told me about his past sooner, I could have been prepared, but no...he didn't think it was the right time. Now look at me! I'm in the middle of nowhere, with a stranger, going to a city I know nothing about, to fulfill some asinine destiny that I am not prepared for! What was he thinking?" Anya's wrath then turned on the only person who was there to hear it. "And *you*," she continued pointing her finger at Koen, "Would it kill you to say two words? Would it kill you to answer a blasted question? Would it kill you to act *human* and realize that I'm scared out of my wits and a little information might, *might*, just help me feel like I'm not walking to my death?"

And that's where Anya ran out of steam. She had to stop talking because her throat had closed up as she tried to hold back her tears. Her last question hung in the air between them. She was exhausted emotionally and physically, but above all she was scared. She knew it wasn't Koen's fault, and that's why after a few moments of silence she knew she needed to apologize. She took a deep, cleansing breath, and prepared her words, but Koen spoke first.

"Your father has a friend, Conley Fitzgerald," he began softly, looking into the flames. "He is the leader of The Council."

"Wait," Anya interrupted in disbelief, "my father knows one of the councilmen?"

Koen looked at her briefly and nodded. "They were friends at The Center." He let that sink in for a moment and continued. "He seems to think that if we can get to The Capital City and talk with Councilman Fitzgerald, he will know exactly what to do."

"But you aren't convinced." Anya could tell by his tone that he was not sure this was the best course of action.

"No," he said after a moment's hesitation. "It has been many years since your father knew the councilman. Much can change in that time, people most of all. I think," here he paused and looked at Anya, almost asking her for permission to continue. At her nod he did. "I think we should approach cautiously. We need information; we need to know what story is being told. The fact that your Mark has appeared means that one of The Council is already dead. We have seen no one this whole trip. Scouts should be scouring the land, looking for you, but they aren't. I find that suspicious." He let that sink in a moment and then continued. "I know people that live in the city, people that I trust. I think it best to go directly to them. It will give us time to hear news and learn the city gossip, before we go barging in to beg an audience with the most powerful man in the city." She thought he was finished, but he quietly continued, "I will leave the decision up to you though, since it is your life."

Anya couldn't easily capture the feeling that flooded through her upon hearing his final sentence. It was a mixture of gratitude, wonder, and power. For the first time, someone was giving her the full story and then handing over the final decision to her. *She* had the control. *She* could decide. *She* had a choice, and it made her feel powerful.

Koen was not at all impatient as she sat and let all that he'd said wash over her. He calmly ate his dinner while he waited for her reply.

"You said two days," Anya asked, "that we would be at The Capital City in two days?"

A simple nod was her answer.

"You will have my decision by dinner tomorrow."

That's when he finally turned and looked at her. He studied her for a moment and she wondered what he saw. Slowly he nodded and turned back to his food.

Anya knew that she should finish eating to keep her strength up, but there was no way that was going to happen tonight. She stood up and mumbled something about being exhausted. It was after she said the words that she realized she really *was* spent. She walked to where she'd arranged her blankets, and paused, "Thank you, Koen," she said softly. She didn't even know if he'd heard her, but she'd needed to say the words. She lay down with her back to the fire, and therefore, never saw the slight smile that spread across his face.

CHAPTER 27

Conley

"It's all clear, Sir. They are ready to walk you to your door."

"Thank you, Noah," Conley said to his driver as he opened his door. As soon as he stood, four guards surrounded him as he walked up to his porch. He sighed. If he was feeling impatient with the increased security, then he knew that Karis and Breanna had to be near to boiling with the extra precautions that had been foisted on them. He was ready to return to some sort of normalcy, but knew that it would be a while in coming, if ever.

Conley closed the door behind him and knew that the four guards would reposition themselves at various points around the house. He didn't envy them their long night. As he completed his routine of securing his briefcase, he wondered why he had even left his office at all. It would only be a few short hours before he had to be up and getting ready for the ceremony tomorrow. He knew it was only the threat of a scolding from Mrs. Martyn that had sent him home. Otherwise, he probably would have just camped out on his office couch.

By now news of the new council member had been "leaked" to the press and public. It was all very controlled, even though it didn't seem that way. This is how it had always been. Some speculation was good; it drew crowds and built anticipation. He still had some of the outlandish articles that were published the week before his own ceremony. He was sure there was some pretty hefty betting going on too. He grabbed one of the papers off his table. Mondry's face was one of several staring back at him. Conley had been right, his classical good looks and natural charisma had made him a fan favorite.

He put down the paper to pour himself a drink. He remembered his own Revelation Ceremony like it was yesterday. He hadn't slept the night before. He spent the time committing to memory the ceremony's order and practicing his speech. Each new Council member was expected to write and deliver his or her own speech. The speech is meant to set the tone for their time on The Council and to introduce the new member to the people. No one, but the newly chosen, is supposed to see or hear the speech until the day of the ceremony. Other Council members could coach him or her, but the final words were completely up to The Chosen. It had been decided that, in Mondry's case, following tradition was especially important. There were only five people that knew him to be a fake, and they needed to keep it that way. Therefore, Conley had given him some intense counseling on his speech, but had not seen the final draft for himself. He, along with everyone else, would hear it tomorrow at the ceremony.

Conley downed the remainder of his drink and headed back to his bedroom. He suspected that, once again, he wouldn't be getting any sleep. Unfortunately that was becoming a common occurrence.

CHAPTER 28

Max

It was when he turned his head that he saw her. She looked as beautiful as always. He loved it when she left her hair down and he could see the strands catch the sunlight. It always had fascinated him with how *alive* it looked. For a moment the thought came to him that she shouldn't be there, but he swatted that aside. It was just too good to see her.

"Mara," he rasped out, "what took you so long?" It was their standard greeting. Whenever they were away from each other, they would greet each other by asking what had taken them so long to get back. It didn't matter if they were greeting each other after a long day at work, or only after a few minutes apart, the greeting was always the same. Max waited for a flippant answer. Once Mara had immediately responded that she had been busy fighting off pirates who thought she was a long lost princess and who were planning to hold her for ransom. She'd told him she was exhausted and expected the best foot rub money could buy. He, of course, obliged. He knew it wouldn't do to make a princess angry.

This time, she said nothing though. She simply stood there, just out of reach, with an incredibly sad look on her face.

"What is it?" Max said as he began to panic. "Are you hurt?" He watched her slowly shake her head. He then felt the sting, as if something was seeking to burrow into his leg. He looked down, trying to find the thing so he could swat it away, but saw nothing. When he looked back to Mara, she was gone.

The next time he awoke he felt something on his forehead. It felt blessedly cool, but was scratchy and irritating. He just wanted it off, but for some reason his arms were too heavy to lift, almost as if they were secured at his sides. *What was going on? Where was he? Where was Mara?*

With super-human effort he opened his eyes. He looked up to see a thatched roof with log crossbeams and supports. He followed the line of the roof down to take further stock of his surroundings. He appeared to be in a small cottage. He felt heat to his left, so he slowly turned his head. He saw a stone fireplace where a pot hung on an iron spit over the flames. Two small stools flanked the fireplace and a wooden table stood nearby. The cottage was small enough for him to see he was alone. He knew he had more questions, but they were starting to get fuzzy. He was just so tired, and hot. If he could just get the blasted blankets off of him, he knew things would clear up in no time. He felt his eyelids getting heavy, he would just close them for a minute, and then he would get up to find out what was going on.

Mara was there. He could feel her presence before he opened his eyes. He gave himself a moment to savor the anticipation of seeing her again. He turned his head and opened his eyes. Sure enough she was there. She didn't look as she had before. This time her hair was in a heavy plait that fell across her right shoulder. This hairstyle always made her look more serious and contained. This was how she looked when she knew she would have a difficult day ahead of her, and she needed as much control over the situation as possible. He loved this Mara just as much as the playful one he often saw. This Mara was an incredible mix of strength and vulnerability, and always reminded him of when he'd first taken notice of her at The Center.

Somehow he knew that she needed him to understand something. This time she sat next to his bed, patiently waiting.

"I don't understand," he rasped. "Just tell me what you need me to know." For some reason she continued to sit in silence, but her gaze grew more intense. He felt the biting pain in his leg, but this time he would not look away from her, for fear that she would disappear again.

He fought against the frustration and fatigue he was feeling. Somehow he knew that she wouldn't be here if this wasn't important. "I'm supposed to remember something, aren't I?" he asked. He felt some satisfaction at her small nod. "Did I forget something from the grocery list again?" He watched disappointment and frustration flood her face. *What was it? What was he forgetting? Think Max.* "If you could just stop whatever is trying to bite my leg off, maybe I could think!" Max told her in frustration.

He saw her face brighten at his words. Okay, that was something. What she wanted him to remember had something to do with his leg. He focused his thoughts there. Why might his leg be hurting so much? It was almost as if his leg was being sliced open. Wait, a knife, yes…he remembered a knife.

"The man in the black coat," he said. He immediately saw her brighten. He was on the right track. "I was protecting something," he continued. "Wait, not something, *someone.*" Yes! He knew he was close. He saw the pride on her face as she rose to stand over him. It was right there, right there on the edge of his memory. Mara gently placed her hand on his forehead and smiled into his eyes. Mara's eyes...they were the same as Anya's eyes...Anya's eyes....Anya! She saw the moment he remembered, her eyes smiled, but he felt a searing pain, this time to his heart. Remembering Anya meant letting go of Mara, and he didn't know if he had the strength to do that again.

"Please," he whispered, "please don't leave me again. I can't..." She leaned back; he could see her eyes flooded with love and pride. He knew she had faith in him, and it was that faith that gave him strength. "I will, Mara. I *will* find her." Her smile was more brilliant than the sun as she leaned forward to place a gentle kiss on his forehead. He closed his eyes, breathing in her familiar scent, and for the first time in five days he slept peacefully.

His fever had finally broken.

CHAPTER 29

Anya

Anya and Koen paused at the edge of the village that would lead them into The Capital City. For the first time in seven days she would be seeing someone other than Koen and she wasn't sure how she felt about that. Koen waited patiently for her indication she was ready to proceed. The night before she had given him her decision about what they would do once they reached their destination. She had gone over every possibility while they had walked yesterday. Finally, after reaching down and letting her senses soak in both possibilities, she knew which option she would chose. She agreed with Koen that their best course of action was to get as much information as possible. Strategically, it was better to go see Koen's friends first.

Anya took a deep breath and stepped out of the woods. Her feelings were a mix of regret and anticipation. She and Koen had worked well together, and eventually had found a rhythm. She had discovered that he wasn't the machine-man she had compared him to that first day. He had a strength and determination that she had never seen before. She came to realize that he communicated most effectively by his actions. He had a strong respect for the land they had traversed, and never did he waste or destroy anything needlessly. He was vigilant in making sure they were secure, and each morning she awoke covered in his blanket. Yes, once she began to notice, she realized that Koen spoke volumes without saying a word. She would miss the comfortable silence that they had shared.

At the same time, she was anxious to get this finished. She was still scared of what may be ahead of her, but she was tired of the anticipation. It was time, and she was ready for whatever awaited her.

"We will walk through the village to the edge of the city. Once there, we can find a tavern where we can ask directions to my friend's house," Koen told her. Anya nodded and fell into step beside him.

For some reason she figured that once they hit civilization, they would stand out like sore thumbs. She imagined that the incredible changes she had gone through in the past week would surely show on her face, that somehow everyone around her could see thorough her clothes to the mark on her shoulder. She realized that she was holding her muscles in tense expectation of being found out, but after making it to the village square without incident, she let herself relax and began looking at her surroundings.

At first glance, this village wasn't much different than those in The Outlands. They'd passed by the blacksmith, butcher, and tannery on the edges of the town where it was less populated. Even here, nobody wanted to be close to those sounds and smells. As they got closer to the square, they saw familiar shops like the bakery and the town tavern. There were differences though. First, everything looked cleaner and newer. The buildings had paint that wasn't chipping and roofs that weren't one stiff wind away from crumbling. Even the people looked fresh and clean, wearing bright colors and clothes that fit well and weren't frayed. Most of the clothing in The Outlands was handmade by the women of the family. All of Anya's clothes were usually payment for some kind of doctoring her father had done. She had always secretly dreaded when he got a call to the

Winchester's farm. Mrs. Winchester was the nicest person ever, but persistently thought Anya was three times bigger than she actually was, and that she had a special love for the color pink. After one or two obligatory wearings, those creations became kitchen rags.

The noise began to pick up as they approached the open market at the center of town. When they passed a stall selling meat pies, Anya's stomach let out a loud growl. She quickly turned to see if Koen had heard. The small upturn of his lips made her suspect that he had, but he didn't mention it other than to say, "Once we get to the tavern we can take the time for a real meal." Her mouth immediately started watering at the thought.

Anya realized they had reached the outskirts of The Capital City when she saw the large number of soldiers patrolling the area. She could feel the tension creep back into her muscles and looked to Koen to see if he was worried.

If anything, he looked curious. "Something is going on," he said. "Let's go in there and have something to eat, and maybe get some information." He pointed to a small tavern called "The Purple Pig". That didn't sound particularly appetizing to her, but she wasn't in a position to be picky.

It was surprisingly light and clean on the inside. Anya looked up to see the lights hanging from the ceiling. She wasn't completely ignorant; she'd heard of electric lights before, but in The Outlands, that was a luxury she had never experienced. It took a moment for her eyes to adjust. After looking around, she had to admit that she preferred natural light. This light was too harsh and jarring; it gave everything an odd color that put her on edge.

"Just two of you?" called a voice from the bar. At Koen's nod the woman yelled, "Just go ahead and sit anywhere. I'll be there in a minute." She then scooted around the counter with a tray of full mugs.

Anya followed Koen to a table close to the kitchen. There were plenty of seats open in a more desirable spot, but Anya knew that this way Koen could keep an eye on everything that was happening in the tavern while at the same time staying close to a back exit if it was needed.

"Come to the big city for the celebration?" the waitress said as she placed two waters on the table.

Anya was about to ask what celebration she was talking about when Koen smoothly said, "Absolutely! We wouldn't have missed it for the world." Anya looked up in surprise at his cheerful tone.

"Exciting isn't it?" the waitress continued. "It's been about fifteen years since our last Revelation Ceremony. I barely remember the last one, so I can't wait to see the whole thing from start to finish. Roger made me work a half day today," she said as she threw a petulant glance behind her, presumably to the mysterious "Roger" and continued, "otherwise I would be camped out at the platform, hoping to get the best spot. It will be broadcast, but that's not the same as actually being there."

Koen made a few sounds of sympathy and said, "We were just heading there when *she* insisted we stop and eat." It took a moment for Anya to realize that she was the "she" he'd referred to. It was then that she began to suspect what he was doing, and although it irritated her that the waitress was now giving Koen a sympathetic look for being stuck with such a shrew, she understood this was the best way to find out what was going on.

"Why don't you give us two of today's specials? That way we won't have to waste time pouring over the menu." It was clear from his tone that the "we" in that sentence meant "she", but Anya just ignored the both of them. It was either that, or make a scene by punching Koen in the face.

"Sure thing," she said with a wink as she trotted off to the kitchen.

"Who are you, and what have you done with Koen?" Anya said as soon as she was out of earshot. She saw the slight flush work its way up his neck. *Good,* she thought, *at least he has the decency to be slightly embarrassed by his behavior.*

He shook his head and leaned over the table to get closer to her. "There' s something more going on here than I'd originally thought. Apparently we are going to see a Revelation Ceremony today."

"Have you ever heard of that?" Anya asked.

"If it is what I'm thinking of," he said, "it is the ceremony that each of The Chosen goes through before he or she takes their place on The Council."

"But how could they have that, when I'm -"

"Anya," he cut her off, looking around sharply, "apparently they found The Chosen."

She was still confused, but knew now not to speak of that in public. How could they have found The Chosen, when she was sitting in "The Purple Pig" waiting on the daily special? Could there have been a mistake? Was there some sort of expiration on The Mark, like if she didn't show up to be "revealed" within a week, someone else was chosen? Absently she reached up with her left hand and rubbed her shoulder. She still felt the welts that marked her as The Chosen. Had they fallen for an imposter? She suddenly felt an urgency to reach the podium and start getting answers for herself.

Koen was watching her intently and arrested her movement when she nearly stood up to leave. "Wait," he said, "wait, we have time. Let's get more information. It is now more important than ever for us to understand what exactly is going on here."

It took every ounce of her will to force herself to calmly sit back down and wait for their food.

CHAPTER 30

Conley

He shouldn't be nervous -- it wasn't *his* Revelation Ceremony -- but he was. He took a deep breath and looked at Mondry. Conley had to admit that he cut a dashing figure. Mondry was bare from the waist up, and although he was tall and lean, he wasn't scrawny. Mondry was in his prime and exuded power with both his physique and his bearing. He wore the loose fitting yellow pants and wide red sash that was customary for this ceremony. As they lined up in order, Conley looked at Mondry's back with a critical eye. Even he, knowing that the symbol there was a forgery, was impressed with how authentic it looked. He was confident that no one would question its validity.

Mondry would be the first out of the doors, followed by The Council and other dignitaries. As soon as those doors opened, Mondry would be revealed to the public as The Chosen. They would then slowly process through the main street to the platform that had been erected for the occasion. From there, the old legend would be read, Mondry would swear his oath, he would give his speech, and the festivities would begin. In years past, The Council would linger and circulate among the people of the city, but this year, things would be different. The danger was not over, and therefore being in public was not safe, especially with so many in The Capital City. There was a car waiting for them at the podium to take them away once the ceremony was complete.

It was time. Conley heard the subtle hush in the crowd just beyond the large oak doors. The trumpeters must be taking their positions. Sure enough, moments later he heard the fanfare that had been played for a century at these ceremonies. He heard Breanna's shaky breath beside him and heard Karis whisper on his other side. "I hope we've made the right decision." It was barely audible, but he could make out the words. She said it almost as a prayer.

The doors were thrown open and he was momentarily blinded by the noonday sun. There was a pregnant pause as the crowd tried to see The Chosen, then an eruption of cheers as Mondry took his first steps beyond the threshold.

CHAPTER 31

Anya

Anya didn't know where to look, at the crowds of people, or at the buildings that surrounded them. After leaving "The Purple Pig" they had continued on towards The Capital City, along with what seemed like the rest of the country. As they got to the edge of the village, Anya got her first glimpse of the city. She wasn't sure what she'd been expecting, but it wasn't quite what she saw.

The Capital City sat at a higher elevation, so one needed to walk *up* to the city, no matter what direction one came from. A large defensive wall surrounded it. The wall itself wasn't the dull granite color of the stone buildings in The Outlands. Instead, it was a brilliant white that reflected the sunlight and made the city stand out even more. The city actually appeared to sparkle in the morning sunlight. The wall was tall enough that many of the buildings beyond were obscured, but she could see a towering, spired building rising above everything else. She could only assume that this had once been the castle of the great king.

They followed the crowd to the main gate of the city. She figured that they would have a hard time getting through, with the number of people flooding in, but the guards were surprisingly efficient. Before long, she and Koen were past the gate and walking along what appeared to be one of the main streets. They followed the crowd up the street, which curved to the right and continued at a small incline towards the middle of the city. The pace of the people allowed Anya the time to take in the buildings around her. The difference between the architecture of the village from which they'd just come, and The Capital City proper, was astounding. It was almost as if they had stepped into a completely different world. The buildings were low with flat roofs and made from the same white brick as the city's wall. Anya figured that people must get lost all the time, because to her, everything looked the same. The streets were narrow, with numerous side streets that traversed the city like a maze.

In no time, Anya and Koen reached the center of the city. It opened into a large circular space. Across the way Anya could see that a platform had been erected for the ceremony. It was elaborately decorated with a flowing yellow cloth as a backdrop and four red banners that displayed rough drawings of The Mark. There were four throne-like chairs along the back edge of the platform and a single podium placed in front of them. It was simple, but impressive nonetheless.

A commotion to the right drew Anya's attention as she and Koen sought to move closer to the platform. It seemed that the crowd there was beginning to part, to make way for some sort of procession. They had arrived just in time to watch the spectacle that was about to begin.

Anya watched as the procession walked up a set of stairs to the right of the platform. Four people filed in, each taking a position in front of one of the chairs. This must be The Council. Anya was incredibly curious about each of them, but her eyes had not left the young man who had led the procession. The minute she had seen him, her whole body had tensed and she'd gotten the metallic taste in her mouth that signaled she was in danger. Her mind sought to calm her senses, but they wouldn't be repressed. She knew, with every instinct she had, that something was not right here. Indeed, something was very wrong, and the blond man with the cold blue eyes was at the center of it. Hoping to calm herself, she pulled her attention from him to the people standing next to him. The woman immediately to his left was an attractive woman with a head of brilliantly red hair that looked as if it would not be tamed. She was petite but not demure. Everything about her radiated life and a vibrancy that was palpable. She wore a brightly colored dress that flowed freely as she moved. Her smile for the crowd looked a bit forced, but Anya liked her immediately.

Anya's gaze traveled further down the row to the next woman, who was a stark contrast to the first. Where the first woman was fire, this one was ice. She was tall and thin, with soft gray hair that was perfectly arranged. The woman was older and wore a beautiful suit -- just a few shades darker than her hair -- that fit her distinguished frame perfectly. Her bearing was intimidating without being off-putting. Anya knew instinctively that if this woman was in your corner, you would have a fierce ally, but if not, you had better look out. She didn't exude warmth, like the first woman had, but she commanded respect, and Anya admired that.

Finally, Anya's gaze settled on the remaining councilman. This must be the Conley that was her father's childhood friend. Physically, he was so different than her father. Where her dad was long and lanky, Conley was built more like a bull. He still retained a muscular build, despite being in his middle years, and although there was a slight graying at his temples, his hair was a thick chestnut brown. She could see what would have drawn her father to him. He had an air of trustworthiness about him and a confidence that didn't tip over into arrogance. There was something else, though, that she couldn't quite put her finger on. She was filled with a sense of unease as she watched him walk forward to the podium.

The crowd was still going wild, and it took him a moment to get them to quiet down so he could begin to speak. Finally, after several more minutes, he leaned forward and began talking.

"People of The Capital City," he began. "Today is a day to celebrate." Here he paused as the crowd renewed their cheering. After a moment he continued, "Although we remain deeply saddened by the passing of our friend and colleague, Councilman Wilcox, we know that he would want us to celebrate his life and legacy." A respectful hush came over the crowd. "Rarely does one have the opportunity to know someone so generous and gentle. Many of you were touched by his work for the city's hospitals and orphanages. He was happiest when he was serving others. He will be missed." Anya knew that last sentence was delivered from his heart. He would deeply miss his friend.

Conley cleared his throat and continued, "Amidst our deep sadness, we do have another reason to celebrate, for with Councilman Wilcox's departure, a new member has been chosen." That last word was almost lost among the cheering of the crowd. Conley had to nearly yell into the microphone as he continued, "According to the ancient tradition, Renae Mondry has been chosen!"

At his words, Anya couldn't help but look at Koen, who had stood stoically beside her this whole time. She noticed a slight tightening around his mouth, and could see the fierce glint in his eyes before a shutter came down to hide his emotions. Anya looked around to the joyous faces that surrounded her. They had no reason not to believe the lie they were hearing. For the first time the thought came to her that this may be a way out of the hand she'd been dealt. No one would ever know if she chose to turn around, leave the city behind, and live a quiet life hunting the woods of The Outlands. As soon as the thought occurred to her though, she nearly gagged at her cowardice. She knew she could never live with herself if she ignored her destiny.

Anya realized that a hush had fallen over the crowd. Conley remained at the podium and appeared to be reading from an ancient scroll. "*.... The Chosen would not always be the best and the brightest of The Storm Children, but instead they would be who and what was needful for their time. It would be made clear who The Chosen were by a mark that would appear on them when the time was right.*" The first time Anya had heard those words, they'd held little meaning. It was just some story that her father was telling her around a campfire. Now though? Now these words held a world of meaning to her. For some reason *she* had been chosen, she was the one that was "needful" at this time. For the first time since this whole thing began, determination outweighed her fear.

CHAPTER 32

Max

Conley looked tired. He'd certainly aged in the last sixteen years, they both had, but there was something more written on Conley's face. Conley had always exuded a quiet strength, but looking at him now, Max couldn't see that as clearly as the fatigue that was written across his face. Once again, he wondered what had happened to Conley that led him to the events of today.

After finally waking from the fever with a clear head, Max had discovered that he and Gus had made it to a village just beyond the gates of The Capital City. Gus had told him that he'd been nearly out of his mind with fever when they'd reached the village. Luckily, Gus was able to find a widow who was willing to rent a small cottage to them so that Max could recover. Gus had finally gotten his hands on some medicine, but he'd feared it would be too late. Finally, after the fifth day, Max's fever had broken.

Max remembered the relief on Gus's face when he'd walked into the cottage that morning to see Max weakly sitting on the edge of the bed, trying to pull his pants on. It took quite a bit of talking, along with the threat of a punch to the face, for Gus to convince Max that he needed to regain his strength before heading out to find Anya. He would be no good to her in his current condition.

While Max had been out of his mind, Gus had been able to gather news and information about what was happening in The Capital City. At first, Gus had thought that Anya and Koen had arrived in the city earlier than expected, and that all of the preparations were for *her* Revelation Ceremony, but it didn't take long for him to realize that was not the case.

Gus's next conclusion was that something had happened to Koen and Anya along the way, that Anya had somehow been killed on her journey and a new mark had appeared. He told Max how incredibly thankful he was that he'd found proof that Anya was alive before Max had woken from the fever. He did not want to greet Max with the news that his daughter might be dead.

When Max had demanded to see proof to the contrary, Gus had pulled out a newspaper showing the pictures of the trainees who were the most likely candidates for The Council. The date on the paper was the same as the morning they all were attacked at their camp by the scout. There is no way they could have known that The Chosen was on her way to The Capital City when the paper was printed. This helped to dampen Max's fears for his daughter, but didn't serve to lessen his urgency to get to her. In fact, it did just the opposite.

The only logical conclusion that Max and Gus could come to was that the one who everyone thought was The Chosen was a fraud. Somehow he or she had gotten past detection and convinced everyone that they were destined to be the newest member of The Council. The question that Max did not have an answer to was whether or not Conley knew of the treachery. The Conley of the past would never have been party to something like this, but Max knew more than most how time and circumstances could change a person. He had to admit to himself that he no longer knew the man who had once been his closest friend.

And now here Max sat, in one of The Capital City's many pubs, watching the spectacle that was happening at the city's core. He took a sip from the strong tea that he'd ordered and looked back at the large screen broadcasting the ceremony. Conley had just finished reading The Legend and was now calling forth Mondry for The Oath.

Max wished he was strong enough to be close to the platform where Mondry stood, although with so many strong emotions in the vicinity, it was unlikely he would be able to get a good read on him. He'd barely made it to the pub without passing out from exhaustion; there was no way he would be able to stand among the crowd. Still, there was something about that young man that didn't sit well with Max. He looked too smooth, too handsome, too confident. Max remembered watching Conley's Revelation Ceremony and thinking about how nervous he'd looked. At the time, Max had to admire Conley for being able to stand upright. Max knew that he'd never have made it through the ceremony without losing his breakfast.

"Oy! Listen up folks," the pubmaster yelled, as he reached over to turn up the sound on the screen. "It's time for his speech!"

The pub suddenly became silent as the patrons stopped what they were doing to give their full attention to the young man on the screen. The camera had zoomed in for a close-up and Max swore he heard the woman sitting next to him at the bar let out a sigh.

"Members of The Council and people of The Capital City," Mondry's smooth voice began. "I thank you for such a warm welcome. I am humbled by your generous acceptance of me as your newest Council member." Max couldn't help but think that he didn't look particularly humble. "As many of you know, I am not like those gathered with me on this platform. I did not grow up in The Training Center, sheltered from the streets of this city. It wasn't that long ago that I, like many of you, was a poor orphan, struggling to find my way in this world. It was the kindness of the citizens of this great city that brought me to this point. It was you who opened your homes to me. It was you who gave of your meager meals. It was you who shared your blankets on the coldest of nights. Now the fates have chosen me to repay those kindnesses. This mark on my back does not simply belong to me, but to all of you as well. We have all been chosen to rise to greatness. We are all special, whether we were born on a stormy night or not. You may look at me today and see someone who has been set apart, but I urge you to look beyond the facade and see a simple man - a man who only wants the best for *everyone* in this great city of ours. I have not, and I *will not* forget that my duty is to all of you."

With that, Mondry turned and walked back to his seat. There was a moment of uncomfortable silence, both in the crowd outside and the one inside the pub. It only took one shout to break the spell of Mondry's words. That one shout though, seemed to grant permission to everyone. The crowd erupted.

Max sat still in the chaos that surrounded him. The people were jubilant. Max now realized the genius of the speech Mondry had just delivered. With a few words he had firmly established himself among the people. He had become their champion. If, and when, he was revealed as a fake, it wouldn't matter. In fact, it would only serve to distance the people further from those in power.

Max looked back to the screen and watched as the camera scanned those on the platform. The other council members looked slightly sick, but tried to hide their feelings behind polite applause. They were well aware of what had just happened.

The camera panned out and swept through the rejoicing crowd. People were dancing in the streets to the music that was now being played through the speakers. It looked as though everyone was enjoying the festivities - everyone except those two.

Max came to attention and focused intently on the screen. The camera had paused briefly on a couple who were not joining in on the celebration, a young woman with dark hair and silver eyes, and a young man with olive skin and black hair. He watched the young man reach down and grab the hand of the girl, pulling her away from the city's center, before they were overrun.

The woman who had been sitting next to Max turned to see his seat suddenly empty. She briefly wondered where the quiet man had gone, but didn't give it more than a passing thought. After all, the pubmaster had just announced a second round of free drinks, and she had some serious celebrating to do.

CHAPTER 33

Conley

"What the hell was that all about, Mondry?" Conley said harshly as soon as they were all safely in the car, headed back through the city to The Council Center. He was too angry to guard what he said. He realized that most of the anger was directed squarely at himself. He should have approved that speech. Hell, he should have written the damn thing himself.

"Conley!" Breanna said sharply.

"What?" he turned abruptly to her. "Were you listening? He did everything but call for revolution right then and there!" Conley turned back to Mondry and pointed a finger at him. "*I* put you here. *I* can just as easily remove you!"

Instead of a look of contrition, Conley saw defiance enter Mondry's cold blue eyes. In that moment Conley realized that this had all been calculated from the very beginning. Mondry had never been a pawn in Conley's game, quite the opposite, in fact. Conley had unknowingly handed over the spade for Mondry to easily plant the seeds of revolution among the people. The enormity of the mistake he'd made hit him full force, but he would not give Mondry another victory today.

As the car stopped in front of The Council Center, Conley turned to Breanna and Karis. "Secure chambers in fifteen minutes," he said shortly. At Karis's raised eyebrow he cleared his throat and added, "please." The both nodded.

They all exited the car. Conley then turned to Mondry and motioned for Captain Hawkins to approach them, "I'm sure after such a taxing morning you are worn out. Please enjoy our hospitality. You will be escorted to the suite we have available for visiting dignitaries. Captain Hawkins will show you the way." It only took a look for Hawkins to understand that he was to make sure that Mondry remained there until further notice. Mondry may have won this battle, but the war? That was another story.

***

The old man had returned to his townhouse almost giddy with excitement. The ceremony had gone perfectly and Mondry had performed better than expected. The tide was beginning to turn, but he needed to keep this momentum. Conley was smart and by now had realized what was happening. He would begin gathering those loyal to the current system of government and start enacting some damage control.

He reached over to the buzzer that was nearby. Within moments, the door to the study opened.

"You needed me, General?"

"Yes, Hobbs," he said. "What is the news from the scout?" It was the silence that greeted his question that pulled his gaze from the window. Hobbs was naturally a timid, mousy looking man, but under the General's gaze he nearly withered.

"Well...um....you see...," the General simply raised his eyebrows, which caused Hobbs to begin wringing his hands. "There's been no word."

The General took a deep calming breath. "Find him," was all that he said.

As Hobbs bowed out of the room, the General resumed looking out the window. It was imperative that he got to The Chosen before The Council did. His fingers absently began turning the ring on his left hand, he needed to make certain The Chosen was never found.

CHAPTER 34

Anya

Koen had a steel grip on her hand and was leading her through the winding streets of the city. Being taller, he had a longer stride than she did, so it felt more like she was being dragged.

"Koen!" she yelled above the crowd. "Slow down!"

"No," was his only reply.

"I can't keep up!" She knew that bordered on whining, but as it was, her choices were either to run or stop all together.

He turned his head slightly and said, "We are almost there."

She had no idea where they were going. After Mondry's speech, they had stood for a moment among the crowd, watching the people celebrate. There had been a subtle shift in the tone of the people. She knew that Koen felt it too when he suddenly grabbed her hand and pulled her into the nearest alleyway.

The farther they got away from the center of the city, the less and less pristine things looked. The buildings they now passed were more rundown. Here people didn't have large beautiful windows to let in the light, or ornately carved doors to add uniqueness to their home. Even the people were more tarnished and lack-luster. Children wandered the streets in ragged clothing and began following Anya and Koen in the hopes of a handout. Adults sat outside their homes, under canopies, and behind stalls where they peddled their homemade trinkets. There was desperation here, desperation like she had never seen in The Outlands.

"It's just up here," Koen said as he sped by yet

another vendor.

Abruptly Koen stopped. Once again, Anya nearly plowed right into him, but she was able to halt herself in time. They stood before a simple wooden door, one that probably didn't do much to keep out the cold winter nights. Koen raised his hand and gave the door a sharp knock. Before someone came to the door, Koen looked at Anya and said, "Say nothing about your Mark." She immediately understood that this was for her protection, so she gave a quick nod just before the door opened.

Anya didn't know what she expected to find behind that door, but the little girl standing before them, was not it. She was a beautiful child, probably around seven or eight years old. She wore a flowing red sundress and had straight black hair that reached her waist. Her eyes, though, were the most arresting. They were a bright clear blue that immediately reminded Anya of the sky back home on a cool spring afternoon, the kind of cloudless sky that grows a deeper blue the higher you look. They were wise eyes that reflected the old soul within.

"We are here to see Luella," Koen said.

The girl closed the door without a word and left them standing on the porch.

"Now what?" Anya asked.

"We wait."

Moments later the girl opened the door once again and motioned them into the house. As soon as Anya stepped over the threshold she was immediately engulfed in the scent of cinnamon and the Laurel leaves that her father would use on some of his patients. The front room was windowless and draped in shadows, with only a single candle burning. Despite the small size of the room, it was nearly filled to over flowing with furniture, which was further cluttered with various trinkets and pillows. When she looked closer, there seemed to be hundreds of small carvings of every kind of animal imaginable. The carvings filled every available space in the room. Part of her itched to spend an hour simply looking at the detailed figurines.

"It has been a long time, Koen, and you have grown much," said a voice from the corner. Anya hadn't even realized there was someone else in the room. She now saw the old woman sitting in a small wooden chair that was wedged between two overflowing end tables. "Come in, come in," she beckoned. "You and your friend are welcome and will find sanctuary here. Jetta," she called, "two chairs for our guests."

Anya watched as the young girl who had shown them in reappeared with two chairs, which she placed near Luella. Anya followed Koen's lead as he deftly wound his way through the room to one of the chairs. It wasn't until they were both seated that Luella spoke again.

"I've been waiting for you to come see me."

Anya expected Koen to reply to her statement, so when he remained silent, she looked up at him. She found him staring back at her. She quickly turned to Luella and met her gaze for the first time. Even in the dim lighting, Anya could see the clear blue of her eyes. Luella seemed to be waiting for something from her, and in her confusion, she turned back to Koen.

"Anya," he said, "Luella is a Seer."

Anya gave a little shake of her head, still not understanding what exactly was going on.

"Koen," Luella said gently, "there are still too many secrets for her to understand. The time has come to grant her some clarity."

That was when realization dawned on her. "Wait," Anya said. "Me? You've been waiting for *me*? You don't even know me!" Suddenly, Anya felt close to tears. She didn't understand any of this. Her world had once made sense, hadn't it? Now, now her world was in chaos. Would she ever know "normal" again? "I don't understand," she finally whispered brokenly.

Luella reached her weathered hands out to lay them gently over Anya's clenched fists. "I have been waiting to see you again, my child," she said. "I've been waiting to meet you since my very first conversation with your mother."

"Again? My mother?" Anya breathed.

Luella seemed to give Anya a moment to let that sink in. Suddenly she turned to Koen and said, "Koen, go help Jetta lift heavy things in the kitchen. This one here...?" she paused, realizing she didn't know Anya's name.

"Anya," Koen supplied at her unspoken question.

"Ah yes, Anya,..... very suitable. Anya," she continued, patting her hands, "is going to help me. It is time for me to gather herbs in my garden."

Koen hesitated, clearly not wanting to leave Anya's side.

Luella looked between them and said gently, "She is protected. No harm will come to her."

"Anya?" Koen asked.

Anya gave herself a small shake and nodded at Koen, "Yes, yes, Koen, it's fine. I will be all right." She wasn't sure if she was trying to convince him or herself. Now that some of the shock had worn off, all she wanted to do was find out what Luella knew of her mother.

Koen nodded and walked toward the back of the house.

"Help me up, girl," Luella said, as she grabbed the arms of the chair she was sitting in for leverage. Anya immediately leaned over and helped her stand. "Over there," Luella pointed, "over there is that cursed cane. I will need that for our walk."

Anya hurried over to where she had pointed, and found the cane leaning haphazardly against a wall. She gave it to Luella and quickly moved out of her way.

"Now, follow me to my garden, and I will tell you the story of your mother."

CHAPTER 35

Max

As soon as Max had seen Anya and Koen on the screen in the pub, he had bolted out of there as quickly as he could. He didn't care if Gus could keep up with him or not, his only objective was to get to Anya before she was lost among the crowd.

He had lived in this city most of his life, and he found that even though he had been gone for sixteen years, very little had changed. He cut through alleyways and even through a few backyards in order to find the most direct route to the center of the city. Once there, he knew exactly how to get to the spot where he'd last seen his daughter. He wasn't polite as he pushed people out of his way, but he didn't care. He could hear Gus calling to him, but he was not going to slow down.

Finally, he reached the spot where the camera had shown them. He turned in circles, calling Anya's name, but they were gone. He had missed them by minutes, he was sure. The adrenaline that had given him the strength to run through the streets, suddenly gave out and he nearly fell to the ground in exhaustion.

Instantly, Gus was there to lift him up. "You fool," he said.

"I saw them, Gus," Max said as he looked down at Gus's weathered face. "I saw Anya and Koen on the screen. They were standing right here."

"Are you sure?" Gus asked.

"I *know* it was them," Max said. "They are here in the city. They made it here." Max's delight in knowing that Anya was alive was short-lived though. "We have to find them, Gus. She isn't safe."

"We will," Gus assured him. "We will. I have a friend, and she will surely be able to help us," he continued, as he helped Max through the crowd, to a small side street that would lead them deeper into the city.

CHAPTER 36

Conley

"You cannot leave him locked away in that room forever," Karis said. Conley, Breanna, and Karis were now all sequestered away in the secure chambers. Conley envied Karis her calm. "Breanna, sit down, your jittering is getting on my nerves," she continued.

Breanna, who had been nervously flitting around the room since they'd arrived, suddenly turned to Karis with fire in her eyes. "*How* can you just sit there so calmly?" Breanna shot back. "We've made a huge mistake by lying about The Mark and bringing Mondry in. What are we going to do?"

"I've..." Conley said.

"What?" Breanna asked, turning to Conley.

Conley finally looked up. "I've," he repeated with more intensity, "*I've* made a huge mistake. *I'm* the one that came up with this plan. *I'm* the one that chose Mondry. *I'm* the one that didn't listen to your arguments, or even my own intuition." Here he rose from the table to stand behind his chair, simply because he needed to move. "*I'm* the one who didn't trust the very system by which our society is ruled. This kind of thing is exactly what this council is designed to prevent." Here Conley seemed to lose steam. He regained his seat, but there was a marked slump to his shoulders. "Breanna," he finished, "*I* am the one who brought this on us all."

"Are you quite finished?" Karis asked.

Conley looked at her and slowly sat up straighter.

"No," he said, "No, I'm not finished." At her raised eyebrows he continued. "I got us into this mess by lying to the people, so I suggest we get out of it by telling the truth. I will resign from The Council." At Breanna's sudden intake of breath, he held up his hand, "Please, hear me out." He could see she wanted to argue, but finally she nodded. He looked over at Karis.

"Please," she said with a slight wave of her hand, "continue."

Conley cleared his throat and repeated, "I will resign from The Council. We will reveal Mondry as the fake he is, and I will take full responsibility for orchestrating the whole thing. From there you will call for a nationwide search for the true Chosen, something we should have done from the very beginning. The whole incident is sure to rock any confidence the people had in The Council and the current system, but if we are honest, I believe that right will win in the end."

After a slight pause to make sure he was finished, Breanna said quietly, "If we follow your plan, you will be tried for treason. You will be tried, found guilty, and executed."

Conley took a deep breath, "Yes, that is the most likely outcome." Conley knew that he could no longer remain a member of The Council, and he knew that no one ever resigned from this position. That wasn't how this worked. The only way that a vacancy was created was when one of the current members was no longer alive. He did not have a death wish, but for the first time in a long while he was seeing the wisest course of action with clarity. Deep down he knew this was the only way.

"There is one major flaw to your plan," Karis finally said.

Conley started to shake his head, "I can't see -- "

"You mentioned honesty," Karis interrupted.

"Yes," Conley agreed, "I believe that, although it will be difficult, honesty will be the key to fixing this."

"Well, your plan isn't honest." He was about to argue, but Karis held up her hand and said, "We allowed you your say without interruption, please afford me the same courtesy."

Suitably chastised, Conley nodded, "Of course, my apologies. Please continue."

"You cannot talk of an honest plan, without including us. This was a Council decision. We are all culpable." Conley saw Breanna nod her agreement out of the corner of his eye. "I will not," here she stopped and looked at Breanna, "*We* will not allow you to bear the full consequences of a decision we made together."

"You aren't suggesting we all stand trial for treason?" Conley asked, "You can't possibly -- "

"I'm not suggesting *anyone* stand trial for treason," Karis calmly interrupted. "Have you learned nothing from what just happened?" Conley knew that she was not expecting an answer to her question. "What was the one thing that drove us to our poor decision and our current circumstances?" Here Karis paused. Conley could think of any number of things: pride, lack of trust, impatience, but he didn't offer any of them. He simply waited for Karis to continue.

"Time," she said, "or more pointedly, our feeling that we were out of it. Did we ever consider there was a very valid reason *why* The Chosen had not come forth? Did we wonder if it wasn't *safe* for The Chosen to appear? Did we remember that somewhere in our midst we were being attacked, and any new member of The Council would become the most vulnerable? Did we bear in mind that there was a greater Plan at work than our own?" Silence filled the room as Karis let her questions sink in. Conley had to admit she was right, he had considered none of what she'd said.

"Everything," Karis spoke softly, "*everything* happens for a reason. Even this. Think about it," here she leaned slightly forward, "we have been handed the best opportunity to discover who is behind this attack against us. We have Mondry." She moved to once again sit with her back against the chair and then continued, "He has passion, charisma, and a very real reason to hate a system that elevates some above others, but he could not have gotten this far on his own. He is a pawn. There is someone bigger, pulling the strings. Release him. Let him scuttle back to the nest that spawned him. Let him lead us to our enemy."

Conley felt a small glimmer of hope start to bloom. Karis was right; before they sought The Chosen, they had to be certain they were ready for him or her, and they had some housekeeping to do before that could happen.

CHAPTER 37

Anya

Anya followed Luella through the back door and stepped into a veritable oasis. Just as her house had been filled to overflowing with furniture and knick-knacks, her garden was bursting with plants of every kind. At first glance the garden seemed completely wild and untamed, but once they started down a path, Anya saw that it was actually organized into a pattern of squares.

"Here," Luella said, handing Anya a tightly woven basket. "We will be needing some of these herbs for our visitors." She slowly hobbled over to a patch in the corner of the garden. Anya easily recognized some of the healing herbs her father would use like chamomile, foxglove, lavender, and rosemary. Back home they actually had a small garden that looked very similar to this portion of Luella's. She wasn't sure what "visitors" they were expecting, and quite frankly she didn't care. Anya wasn't nearly as curious about that, as she was about Luella's mention of her mother. By now she'd gotten over her shock and was impatient to get her questions answered.

Luella slowly folded her small frame to sit on the low stool that Anya now saw stood adjacent to the medicinal herbs. She reached over to pick some of the purple lavender, and then motioned to Anya to hold the basket closer to her. "It means 'bringing goodness' you know." At Anya's look of confusion Luella explained, "Your name, child, Anya means bringing goodness. It is no surprise that she chose that name for you," she said with a soft smile. "Your mother knew that after all the pain and sorrow she'd experienced, you would bring much goodness, to her, and to others."

"How," here Anya hesitated, not sure she should ask questions, or simply let Luella tell the story as she would. "How did you know my mother?" she finally asked.

Luella smiled as she continued picking at the plants. "Your mother would say we'd met by chance, but I know there was no 'chance' involved. Our friendship was woven into both of our destinies."

Anya moved to position the basket closer to where she was working and found it would be easier to simply sit on the ground in front of where Luella sat. Luella placed the flower she had just picked into the basket and paused to look down at Anya. Lifting her hand to Anya's face she said tenderly, "You are very like her, you know. You have Max's hair and lanky build, but everything else is Mara."

Anya had to steady her breathing at Luella's words. Her mother was such a stranger to her that she hungered for any comparison between the two of them.

"How much do you know about your mother?" Luella asked.

"Hardly anything," Anya answered. "My father had just started to share some of his memories of her, but then..." she trailed off, not sure how much of what had happened she should reveal.

Luella turned and stared deeply into Anya's eyes. It made Anya uncomfortable, but she didn't look away. It was almost as if Luella was looking for something. She must have found it because she gave a small nod and went back to her plants. "Yes," she said, "it would be painful and difficult for Max to share her," here she turned back to Anya before she continued, "even with you."

"Your mother came from a powerful family. Her father was a high-ranking official in the government. He sought power and prestige above all else, but with a system such as ours, it was guaranteed that he would never gain a place on The Council, for he was not a Storm Child. He was convinced his only chance would be through a child of his own." Here Luella paused and her voice became harsher, "I will not go into the lengths he went to ensure that a child of his was born during one of the great storms. I will only tell you that his obsession eventually cost his wife's life, something Mara was never able to forgive him for."

Here Luella paused, as if to give a moment of silence for the woman who had lost her life for a madman's dream. She took a deep breath and continued, "Mara was immediately brought to The Training Center as the other Storm Children were. The only difference between her and the others was that, while their parents were only permitted occasional visitations, Mara's father watched over his daughter's progress and training daily. He fully expected her to be the best at everything and to *earn* The Mark, making her a member of The Council. He knew he had no hold over her emotionally, she never felt the need to impress him, and so he turned to harsher methods. He began threatening her friends, or other trainees that stood out. It was when some trainees began to have 'accidents' that Mara started distancing herself from her peers. She hoped by doing this he would have no one to target."

Now the pieces fit together. Anya remembered the story her father had told her about her mother's conversation with the uniformed man. That must have been Mara's father.

"Soon one of the councilmen met with an accident," Luella turned to see the look on Anya's face. "Yes, Mara suspected her father was involved as well, although she never found proof. I'm certain her father thought that she was sure to be the next Chosen, but it was not to be. Instead, Councilman Fitzgerald was marked and became the next member of The Council."

Councilman Fitzgerald, Anya thought, *that was Conley, her father's friend.*

"By then, Mara had met your father. They had been secretly spending time together. Mara tried to warn him that it wouldn't be a good idea to be around her, that her father would most likely harm him in some way, but your father didn't care. Mara's father underestimated Max's influence though. After her father's hopes of getting her on The Council didn't work, she completely cut ties with him and stopped her training all together. She'd always shown an aptitude for organization, so she got a job in the city's planning office. Once she married Max, her father completely left her alone. For the first time, she was free to be who she really was, and your father loved her more for it every day."

Luella had painted such a hopeful picture of Mara's future. Anya imagined that her mother and father had been so happy. She could feel tears prick behind her eyes and a thick lump in her throat. What had gone so wrong?

"You asked how I'd met Mara." Luella sighed and looked off in the distance, remembering. "It was one day, at the city's center market. She'd stopped by my booth, looking at the herbs and spices I had for sale." Here Luella smiled and let out a little laugh, "You should have seen the look of surprise when I suggested she might want some ginger or peppermint, to combat the morning sickness. You see, she'd only told one person, your father, that she was pregnant. She was surprised enough to buy some and hurry home." Anya smiled, too, because she could picture it clearly. "The next week," Luella continued, "when I arrived in the market to set up my stall, she was there waiting for me. She'd guessed that I wasn't only a healer, but a Seer as well. She had so many questions. Instead of answering them, I told her to come here the next day. She showed up right on time. She stayed for hours that day." Anya wondered what they had talked about.

Luella waved Anya over to help her stand. She told Anya to grab her stool and move around to another spot in the garden, "I need some Devil's Claw for the inflammation," Luella mumbled. Anya wasn't sure what she was talking about, but she helped her move to the spot she'd indicated. Once she was comfortably settled she continued the story.

"Mara came to visit me every other week from that point on. She would always begin by asking me to tell her about you; more importantly, she wanted to know about your future. She was looking for assurances that you would not be a Storm Child." Luella turned to Anya at this point and continued, "That was her greatest fear above all. Each time, I would put her off, telling her that the time wasn't right, and it wasn't, not until the very last time I saw her."

CHAPTER 38

Mara
16 years earlier

"Luella?" Mara called from the front door. "Luella? Are you here?" It was her normal time to come and see her, so Mara knew that Luella had not stepped out.

"In the garden!" she heard from the back of the house. Mara smiled. She should have known.

She stepped fully over the threshold of the house. "I brought bread," she called back. She brought a little something else as well. The first time Mara came to Luella's house, she was struck by the amount of *stuff* Luella had fit into her tiny home. The tiny animal figurines she had scattered around the tables and shelves in the front room particularly fascinated her. They were all so different and beautifully carved. So the next time she came, she'd brought a new animal to give Luella as a gift. Mara remembered the delight she'd seen on Luella's face at the tiny elephant Mara had given her. She'd told Mara that it was not necessary to give her gifts, but that she would accept it this one time, in order not to be rude. From then on, it became a game. Mara would always bring a new animal and hide it among all the others. Luella never missed the gift though, because the next time Mara came over, her previous gift would be moved to a new spot. Today she'd brought a tiny owl. She smiled as she gingerly placed the figurine on the edge of the fireplace's mantle.

Mara then walked to the kitchen, to put the bread on the counter, and then continued on to the garden. Oh, how she loved this garden. Having grown up only knowing the city, this patch of land was a haven for her.

She and Max had talked about one day visiting The Outlands, just to see the wilds of nature. She imagined it would be beautiful beyond words.

Mara spotted Luella over by her cooking herbs and headed in that direction. She let out a laugh because being thirty-nine weeks pregnant, she'd gotten so big lately, that walking along the narrow paths of the garden almost became impossible. "What's for dinner tonight?" she asked.

"Stew," was Luella's reply. "How is baby?" she continued without looking up.

"Well, she seems to be a bit restless today," Mara said as she gently rubbed her protruding stomach. "She certainly is strong, don't you think?" she asked slyly. Maybe today would be the day that Luella told her about her daughter's future.

Luella paused and looked up into her friend's face, "Yes, Mara. Yes, your little one is incredibly strong."

Mara sucked in a breath. This was the first time she'd ever answered any questions about the baby she was carrying. Would she be willing and able to tell her more?

Luella grabbed for one of Mara's hands in order to get some help rising to her feet. "Let's go in the house. I want to see what you brought me today."

Mara thought that was odd. They usually spent their time in the garden, but if Luella was willing to talk about the baby, Mara would follow her wherever she wanted to go.

Soon they were settled in the front room. Mara figured it was a minor miracle that her stomach hadn't knocked over any trinkets as she walked to the couch to sit down. Luella settled in a chair near her.

"An owl," Luella said. "You brought me an owl."

"Yes," Mara said with a smile, "I noticed that you didn't have an owl anywhere. I saw this one and just knew I had to get it for you."

Luella took a deep breath, "It is time, Mara. Today you need to know about your baby."

Mara suddenly turned from the owl to Luella. Her tone was serious and brought immediate fear. She felt her heart start to pound. Even the baby went still in anticipation of what Luella was about to tell her.

"I know your fears, Mara. I know what drives your need to keep your child with you and safe from the childhood that you had. In many ways your paths will be very similar. She will experience some of the same losses and fears that you have." Luella waited before she went on, "Like you, she will have the joy and freedom that love brings. Despite the similarities though, there will be many differences." Here Luella leaned forward and placed her hands over Mara's. "Sometimes, some of the very things we do to avoid destiny, are what set it in motion. No matter how much you fight her destiny, it will win in the end."

Mara did not move, waiting for more, waiting for something more substantial. Luella had told her time and time again that knowing too much was dangerous, but couldn't she make an exception in this one case?

"Now," Luella said as she patted Mara's hands, "our time is over." She stood with effort to walk Mara out. "You must go home. A storm is brewing, I can feel it in my bones, and you must spend time with that handsome husband of yours."

Mara gave Luella a strong hug and whispered, "I love you." She turned quickly and hurried out the door. She needed Max.

It was as she turned the last corner before their

house that she simultaneously heard the low rumble of thunder in the distance, and felt the first labor pain.

CHAPTER 39

Anya

"That was the last time I saw Mara," Luella said gently. She seemed to come back to the present and notice that Anya was there listening to her story. "That was the night you were born, and the night your mother died."

It was like a punch to the gut to Anya. *She? She* was the cause of her mother's death? It was *her* fault that she had been taken too soon? She had never asked her father about how her mother had died. Her mother was a topic they never talked about. She knew from a young age that it was painful for her father when she asked about her mother, so eventually she stopped asking. She couldn't say she'd never been curious about her mother's death, but she knew better than to ever voice those questions. She wished she could go back to her ignorance; it was far less painful than realizing *she* was responsible for her mother's death. How did her father not hate her? The devastation she felt was total, complete, and clear on her face.

"No!" Luella said sharply. "No, Anya, it was not your fault. This was a choice your mother made."

"How is dying in childbirth a *choice*?"

"It was by her insistence that Max did not call a midwife," Luella told her. "She knew that you would be catalogued and taken to The Training Center. You were born amidst the worst storm we'd seen in decades. She *knew* the power and destiny that storm would impart. She *made* Max promise to not call anyone and to get you to The Outlands as quickly as possible."

"How did he...?" Anya could only imagine the

devastation that her father experienced that night. She wanted to know how he had fulfilled Mara's wishes, but didn't know how to ask.

Luella understood. "He brought you to me," she said quietly. "That was the only time I had ever met him. I opened my door to find a young man, dripping from the storm, carrying a baby. His eyes told me who he was, and what had happened. He left you with me and went to see to Mara." Luella waited a moment before she continued quietly, "He told everyone that you both had died. He came back the next morning to get you, and left that afternoon for The Outlands."

Anya sat still and frozen, almost afraid to move. She looked up at Luella, with pain in her eyes and asked, "How does he not hate me?"

"Because you are our daughter, and she is alive through you." Anya spun around at those words and saw her father standing there. She was in his arms before she realized she was moving.

CHAPTER 40

Max

Max would have done anything; in fact, he had done *everything* to spare Anya this pain, but he knew she'd needed to know the truth. He felt her heartache as if it were his own, which indeed it was. He mourned Mara every day, and now his daughter mourned with him.

"You aren't angry with me?" Max whispered.

Anya leaned back and looked up at him. "Angry? Why would I be angry?" she asked.

Max lifted his hands and smoothed the hair away from her face. It was like looking at Mara. He'd never paid much attention to that before, maybe he'd blocked it because he was afraid of the pain it might bring. Instead, looking at their daughter, all he could feel was happiness that Mara lived on in Anya. "Because I kept her from you all these years," he said simply.

Anya's face softened, "I can't say that I always understood, but I do now." She took a deep breath and a step back. "How did you find me? You look too thin. What happened to you? Where's Gus? Has Koen seen you?"

Max interrupted her stream of questions with a laugh. *This* was his Anya. "Whoa! Slow down there."

Anya grabbed his arm and placed it over her shoulders while she moved her arm to support his back. "Luella?" Anya asked. "Were those herbs for *this* visitor?"

Max had forgotten that the old woman had been sitting in the garden this whole time. He moved to let go of Anya so that he could help Luella walk back to the house, but was quickly reprimanded.

"I think that you need much more help than I do, young man!" She said with a huff. "Anya, bring him into the house before he gets another fever. I need to look at that leg."

Anya and Max dutifully followed behind Luella as she brought them back into the house and directed them to a small bedroom next to the kitchen.

"And take those pants off," they heard Luella yell from her herb pantry. Max could feel the blush rising to cheeks.

"Do you need help?" Anya asked.

"No!" he said, "No, I will be fine. You go in the front room to hear our tale of woe from Gus."

With a kiss to his forehead, she quietly walked out the door.

Max couldn't believe their luck. When he and Gus had left the square, Gus had told him that he had a good friend, a fellow Seer, who lived nearby. They would go to her and maybe, with their combined efforts, they would be able to find Anya.

Max hadn't paid much attention to the route they took, but as soon as he was standing on the porch, he was taken back to that awful night sixteen years ago. "Luella," he had whispered.

He recalled how Gus had started with surprise, and then shook his head saying, "I should not be surprised at the workings of fate." Gus had knocked on the door and they had both gotten a shock to see Koen standing there.

Max had pushed past him and as he frantically searched the house for Anya, he overheard Gus say something else about fate. When he had finally reached the kitchen he had begun to panic; what if she and Koen had gotten separated? But then something out the window had caught his eye. He had drawn closer to see the old woman sitting with Anya at her feet. They looked to be in an intense conversation, paying no attention to what might be happening around them.

His stomach had churned; he had known Luella was telling Anya about Mara and his immediate reaction was fear. Slowly, he'd walked out into the garden and up the path to where they sat. He was directly behind Anya when he'd heard her question, *How does he not hate me?* The pain and sorrow that had rolled off of her had hit him like a wave and he'd spoken without thinking.

His thoughts were interrupted when Luella came in the door after a quick knock. "Now," she said, "let's take a look at that leg."

When she left, he was exhausted. He suspected that there was a bit of a mild sedative in that tea she'd given him. He wasn't angry though; as a physician, he knew that rest was the best for him right now. Anya was here. She was safe. He could sleep peacefully knowing that was enough for now.

CHAPTER 41

Anya

Anya lifted the tiny figure of the owl that had been resting on the mantle above the fireplace. She'd been looking at all the animals that filled Luella's front room for the last half hour. She told herself that she was just curious about the workmanship of them all, but as soon as she saw the owl, she admitted that she'd been hunting for this particular one. She held it in her hand and closed her eyes, hoping to feel some sort of connection to her mother through the figurine.

"There certainly are a lot of them, aren't there?" Koen said.

Anya jumped slightly, and wondered how long he'd been standing there. Slightly embarrassed, she nodded as she replaced the owl on the mantle. She took a deep breath and realized that suddenly she felt incredibly closed-in. She had the overwhelming need to get out into the open air.

"Let's go," she said to Koen, as she rushed past him.

"Wait!" she heard Koen say after a moment of surprise, "Wait, where are you going?"

He caught up to her as she reached the door, and halted her with a hand on her arm.

"I need air," she said as she turned her wild eyes to him, "I need to walk. I just need," here she paused, looking for the right word, "out."

He searched her face a moment and then nodded. "Just let me tell Gus where we are going. Will you wait for me?"

It was only once Anya nodded that he let go of her arm. She took a deep breath as she watched him walk to the back of the house.

He was back within moments. "Okay," he said opening the door for her, "lead the way."

She stepped out onto the porch and looked to the right and left. What she really wanted was the woods, with the great trees and green foliage of The Outlands. The play of sunlight and smell of the damp earth had always calmed her when she was upset, but looking at the crowded street before her, she knew that would not be an option.

She wondered if looking at some of the wares people on the street were selling might serve as another way to distract her thoughts. She turned to the right, going up the street they had come down only a few hours ago.

The light of day was starting to fade, but the streets were still crowded with merchants. Anya walked slowly, looking at what the people had for sale. Their treasures ranged from beautiful hand-painted scarves and clothes to unique jewelry. When they had sped past earlier, she'd figured that most of what was for sale was cheap, not well made, but what she saw now told her differently. She slowed even more to admire the workmanship that had gone into everything that these people had crafted. The items were beautiful and whispered of the time and talent it took to create them.

The closer she looked, the more she realized that people were not simply selling their goods along the street, but that they were busy making them as well. She stopped, fascinated by one woman as she sat spinning a brightly colored yarn. She watched as the wheel she was working at spun and twisted the wool that the woman so expertly drafted. The rhythm seemed incredibly soothing to Anya, and she envied the woman's simple task.

Anya continued on further down the street, stopping periodically to admire the wares laid out before her. Soon she became comfortable enough to complement some of the artisans on their work and to ask about the techniques they used to craft their goods.

All the while, Koen walked near her. He gave her the space she needed, but always kept her in sight. She was thankful for that, because it was just what she needed. She needed the freedom to roam where she would, but understood that protection was necessary as well.

With each step, Anya could feel the tension beginning to leave her. For the first time in so many days she wasn't walking toward a destiny or dredging up family secrets. For the first time in a long while, Anya was simply enjoying the moment, with no thought of what may come.

Anya stopped to admire a beautiful piece of cloth that was a lovely mixture of bright jewel tones. She was fascinated by the way the reds so naturally bled into the purples and blues. She looked up and smiled at Koen, who was a few stalls away, talking with a man about the intricate metal works he had for sale. He caught her eye and returned her smile with a slight shrug. She chuckled as she brought her attention back to the scarf in her hand.

"That would be the perfect complement to your eyes." Anya looked up in surprise at the low voice that spoke to her. The black eyes that greeted her set her heart pounding and immediately brought her back to the day when she had first seen this man, the day he had walked into their camp wearing his long black coat and brandishing a knife.

"It's so good to see you again, Anya," she heard him say before pain exploded on the side her head and her world went black.

CHAPTER 42

Max

Max came awake slowly and stretched languidly. He hadn't felt this rested in quite a while. He tried moving his leg and found that much of the pain was gone. One look told him that the gash was no longer an angry red and that much of the inflammation was gone. He would have to have a long conversation with Luella to pick her brain about what herbs she'd used.

He sat up and reached for his clothes at the foot of the bed. He wanted to get dressed quickly. He was sure, by this point, that Anya had heard all about his journey to The Capital City, but he wanted to know what *her* travels had been like. They also needed to regroup and come up with a plan as to what they would do next. First though, he wanted to get some food. For the first time in days, he was starving.

He left the bedroom and found that the house was curiously quiet. He walked from room to room and finally found the others gathered in the front room. The minute he walked in, he felt the tension. They didn't notice that he was there as he assessed the situation. Worry, fear, and anger all flew at him at once. Luella was sitting on the edge of her seat, deeply worried, while Gus and Koen both stood nearby. Gus was trying to calm Koen, who looked nearly wild. Everyone was there, everyone except Anya.

"Where is Anya?" he asked. Everyone immediately turned to him in surprise. He saw the panicked look that was tossed between Gus and Luella.

Koen stepped forward and said, "He got her." At his words Max's gut twisted and his throat closed. He did not have to question who the "her" was. "I let my guard down," Koen continued. "I never thought...I thought she was safe," he said as he ran his hand through his hair in a gesture of frustration.

As the meaning of Koen's words hit him, Max reacted as a father first and nearly flew across the room at Koen. When he checked his movements, he then clearly felt the self-disgust and anger that were coming from Koen. "Tell me," Max said tightly.

Koen took a deep breath and began pacing in the small amount of room that was available to him. "She said she'd needed air, that she needed to get out for a while," he started. "I thought it would be all right. No one knew her, she looked so lost," here he looked at Max, hoping he understood. At Max's nod, Koen continued, "She just wanted to wander around the street, looking at all the things the people were selling. She seemed so fascinated by it all, and I could see the tension start to leave her." Here he paused for another breath, almost trying to process himself what had happened. "She was just fine....she was looking at a scarf..." He shook his head, "It was so fast, one minute she was there, smiling at me, and the next..." Here he finally looked up at Max, "I tried to follow them," he said desperately. "There were so many people. I couldn't get to them. I looked. I *searched,* but they were gone." Max could feel Koen's need to have him believe that he'd done all he could to get her back. "It was *him*. It was the scout from camp that day. He found her and he took her."

Max gave a curt nod and immediately knew what they needed to do. "You," he pointed to Koen, "get any weapons you have with you." Koen gave a second's pause before he nodded and went off to find his pack.

"You two," Max said as he reached down to write something on the pad of paper by the door, "You two start trying to find Anya." Both Luella and Gus nodded as Max handed Luella the piece of paper. "Koen and I will be at this address. If you discover anything, get the information to us."

Max turned to leave, he needed a few more things to gather before they left, but he paused and turned back to Luella. "Find her," he said with every bit of desperation he was feeling. "Find her...please." Luella nodded as he spun around and headed off to find the one person he knew who could give him some answers.

CHAPTER 43

Conley

Conley had given his guards the night off. He was tired of their constant presence, and he knew that they simply wanted to enjoy the celebrations that would carry on through the night. After the council meeting, he had met with Captain Hawkins to discuss putting a tail on Mondry. As soon as that was in place, they had let Mondry go. Mondry had been surprised, but he wasn't a fool. He knew that Conley wouldn't simply let him go without keeping tabs on him. Despite that, Conley had no doubt that Mondry would lead them to whoever it was that was behind all of this. He knew that Mondry believed that he could shake any tracking that was put on him. Therefore, they'd put many safeguards in place to make sure that didn't happen. He knew that Mondry was arrogant enough to believe he still had the upper hand.

As Conley walked into his house, he suddenly felt incredibly weary. Tonight, he probably would be able to sleep, simply from mere exhaustion. He took a deep breath and headed to his study to secure his briefcase.

The room was in shadows, despite the drapes being open to the bright moon that shown outside. He walked across the soft rug to his large mahogany desk. It was the soft click of the door closing that alerted him to the fact that he was not alone. He'd had enough training, though, to not give away the fact that he'd heard. Without a hitch in his movements, he reached for the phone that was on his desk, and the panic button that was connected to The Council's Guard.

"Don't," he heard a man say. "Raise your hands

slowly, and turn around."

Now Conley hesitated, deciding whether it was worth the risk to get to the button.

"I wouldn't if I were you," the voice said. "No one has to get hurt."

Conley wasn't sure if he believed him, but he decided to do what was asked of him anyway. He slowly raised his hands and turned to face the threat.

Two men stood in the shadows. He couldn't make out their faces or if they had any weapons, so he waited for what would come next.

"Where is she?" the voice demanded.

Now, Conley was completely confused. *She?* "I don't know-" he'd started to say.

"Don't lie to me!" the man angrily demanded as he stepped out of the shadows. "Where is Anya?"

"Max?" Conley breathed. He couldn't believe what he was seeing. Max. It had been a lifetime since he'd seen his friend. He looked so familiar, and yet so different. Conley took in everything about him. He hadn't changed that much, on the surface, but the angry look in his eyes was one that Conley had never seen there before. Something was not right. His confusion grew even greater. What was Max doing here?

"Max? Max, why are you here?" Conley said as he started to lower his hands.

"Enough!" Max yelled. "We don't have time for this. I will take her far from here and you can do whatever the hell you want with the politics of this damn city. Just tell me where she is."

Conley took a deep breath and spoke slowly, "Max, I don't understand. I don't know anything about someone who is missing." He could tell that Max was about to insist again so he spoke quickly, "Max, I *know* you can tell what I'm feeling."

Max paused and was quiet for a moment. Conley could see the moment that Max believed him. Max seemed to deflate right before his eyes.

Conley's gaze was momentarily drawn the second man, who had taken a step towards Max. Although he was tall and powerfully built, Conley realized that he was young. Conley's concern was Max though, so he brought his attention back to him.

"Max," he said, as he took a step forward, "tell me how I can help you."

"I was convinced," Max said, "I was convinced it was you, that you had her."

"Who?" Conley asked, "*Who* did you think I had?"

"Anya," Max said as he looked at Conley, "my daughter."

Conley was now even more confused, but he no longer felt threatened. He knew Max, and he knew that Max would not harm him. "All right," he said as he walked over to close the drapes and turn on the light, "I still don't know what you are talking about, but you are going to fill me in." Conley walked over to the sideboard, where he kept a decanter of brandy and started pouring a glass for Max. "Sit down, Max."

"We don't have time for a visit and a drink," Max said. "If you don't know where she is, that's fine, but we aren't going to sit around here doing nothing while they have her." Max turned to head towards the door and added, "Come on, Koen."

"Wait!" Conley said sharply. "I have the city's best resources at my disposal. I can help you find her."

Max hesitated.

"Just answer me one question," Conley said. "Why did you think that *I* would have taken her?"

Max turned back to him and said quietly, “Because she is The Chosen.”

CHAPTER 44

Anya

The first thing she felt was the incredible pain in her head. She was confused. *Why* was her head hurting so badly? She had flashes of memory, but no recollection of where she was or what she had been doing. She was having trouble holding on to a thought; the pain kept intruding. One thing she did know, there was an urgency that told her she was in trouble.

She gave herself a moment and then began concentrating on her current situation; maybe that would tell her what she needed to know. Without opening her eyes, she realized she was sitting in a hard chair. Her arms and legs were restrained, with what, she wasn't sure. She didn't hear anything, but somehow she knew she was not alone in the room.

"You aren't what I'd expected," a quiet voice said. Apparently, he had been watching closely for her to wake up, and when he saw her stirring, he decided to let her know he was there.

Suddenly, she remembered. She remembered The Mark. She remembered her journey to The Capital City. She remembered the Revelation Ceremony. She remembered Luella and hearing the story of her mother. She remembered walking through the streets with Koen. She remembered the man in the black coat.

Slowly she opened her eyes, afraid that the light would make her headache worse. She knew, somehow, it was important to analyze where she was. She had to concentrate, to find a way out if she could.

The light was dim, but she could see well enough to recognize that she was in some sort of study. It was richly furnished with dark woods and deep colors. She was situated in the middle of the room, with two long couches on either side of her. In front of her was an impressive desk, and to her left a wall of shelving, filled with books. She didn't turn her head, but presumed that her back was to the door. To her right was a large picture window that looked out to the lights of the city beyond. In front of the window sat a man in a wheelchair.

She couldn't tell much about him, because he was facing away from her looking out the window, but she noticed that despite the wheelchair, he sat tall and erect. He was wearing some sort of jacket with a heavy golden braid, which hung from his shoulder and passed under his arm. She realized that it must be some kind of military uniform because she'd seen similar jackets worn by the guards in the city. She wasn't sure what color his hair used to be, but now it was almost a pure white.

"I expected someone," here he paused, looking for the right word, "stronger. I imagined that The Chosen would be someone a bit more *impressive.*" He let out a derisive laugh. "This is exactly why this system doesn't work," he continued as he began to wheel the chair around the couch that separated them. "Who, in their right mind, would choose a little girl," he sneered, "to rule?"

His voice alone made her skin crawl, but his words and tone made her blood boil. He finally positioned himself directly in front of her. "I'm really doing you a favor, you know," he told her. "You wouldn't last a month on The Council."

Until then she had kept her head lowered, but his

contempt brought her face up. She did not try to hide her own disgust. "You know *nothing* about me," Anya said fiercely.

For a moment the sneer on his face turned to one of complete shock. She heard his intake of breath and his whispered, "It can't be..."

Her brow wrinkled in confusion, until he leaned forward and she could see his face clearly. She heard her own intake of breath when she met an identical pair of silver eyes looking back at her, and realized she sat tied to a chair in front of her grandfather.

CHAPTER 45

Max

Max was growing impatient. He was afraid that Anya was running out of time. For all he knew, she could already be dead. They were wasting precious minutes answering all of Conley's questions.

"I told you," Max said, "my daughter didn't die with Mara that night. I hid her away and the next day we left for The Outlands."

Conley sat in one of the armchairs in the room. The shock of hearing Max's explanation for the second time did not seem to be wearing off.

"Why Max?" Conley said with a shake of his head. "This all could have been avoided if you would have just -"

"It doesn't matter right now!" Max burst out.

"You are right," Conley said with a slight shake to his head. He rose to his feet and walked to his desk." Tell me everything about her abduction."

Max had gone over it and over it in his mind, but he hoped that with Conley's wisdom, he might be able to find something that they had missed. "She was on the street in Quadrant Four."

"The artisan's quarter?" Conley asked.

"Yes," Max replied. "She was outside one of the stalls when a scout took her."

"A scout?" Conley asked. "How did you know that it was a scout?"

Max began pacing as he explained. "He came into our camp the morning after Anya's mark appeared. He must have followed us for some reason." Here, Max began to pinch the bridge of his nose to stave off the tension headache he could feel forming. "I remembered him talking to me in the village the day before. He'd asked a lot of questions and I could tell he was looking for information. He was the reason, along with the questions that Anya had started asking, that we headed up into the mountains in the first place. He made me nervous and I knew I needed to get Anya far away from him." Max paused, remembering the panic he felt that morning when he turned to see the scout standing just inside their camp. Now, just as it had that morning, his fear for Anya nearly overwhelmed him.

"He appeared in our camp. It was clear that he was after Anya, and that he'd heard enough during the middle of the night to know that she'd received The Mark." Max stopped pacing and looked at Conley. "I suspected that if The Chosen hadn't been located, you would have sent scouts looking for them, but he was different. He mentioned an employer. After he took her, I assumed that employer was you."

"Me?" Conley said, clearly shocked. "Why would you assume it was me?

Max could feel the hurt in Conley's words. He could feel the pain that Conley was experiencing as he realized that Max thought him capable of orchestrating all of this. Max looked at Conley full in the face. "I saw the Revelation Ceremony. I *knew* Mondry was a fake. I also knew that you were too sharp not to catch it. The only conclusion I could come to was that you had set the whole thing up." Here Max sighed, "We all change Conley. The Conley that I knew would never abduct The Chosen for their own schemes, but then again, he never would have been party to the farce I witnessed this afternoon either." Max paused and let his words sink in,

"I no longer knew you."

Conley simply nodded, accepting this consequence of his actions. "All right," he said, "you said he mentioned an employer. Were you able to get any more out of him?"

"The only other information we were able to get was the picture of a signet ring," Max answered.

"What did it look like?" Conley asked.

"It was a gold ring, with the picture of a set of arrows bound together with a serpent engraved on the top."

Suddenly a light entered Conley's eyes and he rushed over to his bookshelves. He took to search out the book he was looking for. "Here it is," he said when he found it. He brought the book back to his desk and began paging through it. Koen and Max rushed over to see what he was searching for.

"Here," he finally said, as he pointed to a symbol on the page. "Is this the symbol?"

Max looked closer. The symbol that Conley was pointing to was exactly as Max had described. It was a set of six arrows held together by a coiled snake. "It sure looks like Gus described," Max said.

"Gus?" Conley asked. "No, never mind, it doesn't matter. If this is it, we may have a bigger problem then we first thought" He grabbed the page that the symbol was on and tore it out of the book.

Before Max could ask what he meant by that, they heard a knock at the front door. All of them froze and looked at each other.

"Wait here," Conley said as he strode forward to head to the front door of his house. Max and Koen moved closer to the open study door to listen, in case they were needed.

Conley was back quickly with a small piece of paper in his hand. “It’s a message for you,” he said as he gave it to Max.

“Luella,” Max said, reaching for the paper, “she must have found Anya.” Max desperately unfolded the paper and walked towards the light to see better what message Luella had sent.

“What does it say?” Conley asked.

“No,” Max whispered. His face had gone ashen when he read the two words that were printed on the paper. “‘The General’,” he whispered. “The paper just says, ‘The General’.”

With those two words Max knew exactly who had Anya.

CHAPTER 46

Anya

Anya realized that her grandfather knew who she was, but before he could ask her any questions, there was a commotion outside the doors of the study. Her grandfather's eyes narrowed as the door flew open.

"I don't care *what* he said," came an angry voice. "He will see me."

Anya could hear some sort of scuffle and then heard the door slam.

"Don't you think I should have known about this?" the man said as he walked past Anya to have a seat on the couch to her right.

Anya hadn't turned her head when he'd entered. She was more curious to watch her grandfather's reaction to the person who spoke so arrogantly to him. Now, though, she slowly turned her head and locked eyes with the young man she'd first seen this afternoon at his Revelation Ceremony. This time, he was dressed all in black, which added to his menacing appearance. His golden hair reflected the light in the room, nearly giving him a halo. The contempt in his eyes perfectly matched the sneer on his lips. Her instincts about Mondry had not been wrong this afternoon. Once again, all her instincts warned her against him.

"*This* is it?" he said with a wave of his hand towards Anya. "Wow, maybe we should just give her to The Council. They would take one look at her and *beg* me to remain."

As soon as he had started to talk, Anya turned

away from him. She knew that her grandfather had been watching her closely, to see her reaction, but she'd barely heard what Mondry was saying. She was too busy employing all her energy trying to figure out the best way out of the situation she'd found herself in.

"I wouldn't be so sure," was her grandfather's quiet reply.

This brought two pairs of young eyes back to the old man.

"*What?*" Mondry said. "Are you kidding me?" At her grandfather's words Mondry sat up, no longer lounging comfortably.

Out of the corner of her eye, Anya saw his head swivel back and forth between her and her grandfather. He was beginning to realize that something else was going on.

Anya was still closely watching her grandfather, so she saw the maniacal gleam enter his eyes.

"It seems that The Fates did see fit to reward me for all of my work for this city." He started to laugh. "Oh, wouldn't Mara hate this?" he said as he laughed even harder.

"What the hell are you blathering about?" Mondry nearly yelled. "Who the hell is Mara?"

At the mention of her mother, Anya's eyes narrowed. She knew, she *knew* what he was thinking. In that twisted mind of his, he thought that her being chosen was some sort of reward for everything he'd done. He now saw a different way to power - through his granddaughter.

"Watch your tone, boy," her grandfather said sharply. "You aren't nearly as valuable as you once were."

Anya noticed the stillness that suddenly settled on Mondry. For the first time since he barged in the door, he held his tongue and waited for her grandfather to continue.

"Mondry," her grandfather said, "I'd like you to meet my granddaughter."

Now Mondry's blue gaze flew to Anya and instead of dismissal, she saw appraisal in them. A new calm had settled over him, and to Anya that was much more concerning to her than his arrogance had been. "How?" he asked in a measured voice.

"I have no idea," her grandfather chuckled, "and frankly I don't really care."

"How do you know for sure then?" Mondry asked quietly.

"If you would have known Mara you wouldn't be asking me that question." he said, as he wheeled himself around to his desk. "She may have the hair of that ill-bred fool Mara decided to marry, but her face is all Mara, even down to the look of hate she is shooting me right now."

Anya tried to school her features to reflect nothing, but she suspected it wasn't working. She'd already realized that the best way for her to survive this was to play upon her grandfather's obsession with a family connection on The Council. She knew that it wouldn't take much convincing on her part to make him believe that she was willing to be his puppet. The problem was that she wasn't sure if she could do it. Even knowing the words would be lies, she didn't think she'd be able to get them past her lips.

Her grandfather had been looking for a piece of paper on his desk and mumbling while he did so. Every once in a while he would add a laugh. Anya realized that at some point over the years, madness had completely taken over his mind.

"Ah, yes," he finally said, "here it is." He placed the large piece of what looked like parchment on his lap and rolled his chair back around the desk towards Anya. "I will show you, my girl. I will show you that we are *destined* to rule here."

By now Mondry was standing. He moved slightly so that he could see over her grandfather's shoulder. Anya was curious as to what was on the paper, but she also knew that she needed to keep her eye on Mondry. He was too quiet. Like a leopard waiting to pounce, he was too still, and it was making her nervous.

"Do you know what this is?" her grandfather asked. He didn't wait for an answer. It was almost as if he was talking to himself. "This is my," here he paused and smiled, "I mean *our* family tree. Do you see?" he asked, pointing to the paper. "Do you see how far back we go?" He pulled the paper back towards himself so he could study it. "I knew as soon as I saw this the first time so many years ago that my calling was to make sure that a great wrong would be righted." Finally, he pulled his attention away from the writing on the paper to look up at her. He leaned forward slightly and almost whispered, "We are descended from kings, my dear. We are Margrave's legacy, and we shall regain his throne."

CHAPTER 47

Conley

Conley vaguely remembered Mara's father being some sort of general in the military while they were at school. He didn't really think too much about it though, because most of the trainees didn't remain connected with their birth families. It was the nature of things that your real family became the friends you grew up with at The Training Center.

As soon as Max had told him who he thought had Anya, Conley ran to his desk phone to call Captain Hawkins. At the same time, he opened his desk drawer to reveal the stash of knives he kept there. He began strapping them to his body as he waited for Hawkins to pick up his call.

As soon as he identified himself, he heard Hawkins say, "We were just about to call you, Sir. Mondry is on the move."

"You can tell me about that in a moment," Conley said quickly. "I need an address. I need you to find out where General Evans is staying."

"One moment," was Hawkins's efficient reply.

Conley could see Max's impatience, but he also knew that it would be no use wandering the city looking for General Evans. Even with an address, Conley was well aware that it might not be the place where they were keeping Anya.

"Sir?" he heard Hawkins say through the receiver.

"Yes," he said as they all brought their attention back to the phone call.

"General Evans is staying in Quadrant One, Street E, house number 35," Hawkins reported. That was a mere two blocks from Conley's house. They could be there in minutes.

"Thank you, Hawkins," Conley said as he moved to replace the receiver.

"Sir!" he heard Hawkins yell, before he could hang up.

"Hawkins, I really don't have -" Conley started to say.

"Sir," Hawkins said sharply, "You need to know." Hearing the commanding tone from Hawkins, Conley tampered his impatience, realizing whatever he had to say was important. "*That* is the exact address that we've tracked Mondry to. Mondry and General Evans are together."

His panicked eyes flew to Max. Max had told him enough for Conley to know that there was a good chance the general would realize Anya was his granddaughter, and as The Chosen, he now had a stronger connection to The Council. Mondry would soon realize that General Evans no longer needed him, and that Anya was a threat to his bid for power.

"Get people there," Conley commanded into the phone before he dropped it on his desk not waiting for a reply.

He looked at Max and Koen, "Now," he said as he ran past them. "We need to get to her *now*."

CHAPTER 48

Anya

"You've completely lost it, old man," Mondry said quietly. In this instance, Anya had to agree with him. Her grandfather's thirst for power had gone far beyond the edge of reason.

"No!" her grandfather barked. He seemed to catch himself, and after a deep breath, he continued with more control, "No. No, Mondry I may be the sanest one in this whole city. What is more asinine -- believing that a magical being came to a king and decided that power would be granted to people through storms? Or, that it is the *right* of a king's heir to rule in his place? Don't you see?" Here he turned to Anya, "The kingdom could once again be how it was meant to be. With *you* on The Council, we could take back what rightfully belongs to us."

"And what of me?" Mondry quietly asked.

"You?" her grandfather scoffed. "You were never more than my puppet." His eyes turned cold and hard as they looked up at Mondry. "You are nothing more than a low-born commoner that I plucked from the streets. You should be grateful for the time you had - for the time *I* gave you." Her grandfather shook his head and with a wave of dismissal said, "I don't need you anymore."

Anya saw how confident and arrogant her grandfather was in his disregard of Mondry. She imagined that, in his prime, he had been an intimidating force, accustomed to being feared and respected. What he failed to realize, was that he was no longer in his prime. He was a delusional old man in a wheelchair, and that's what Mondry saw as well.

"No, old man," Mondry said quietly. He slowly leaned forward, so that his face was close to her grandfather's, with their noses almost touching. Anya watched as Mondry brought his hand to his back and took something from his waistband. She saw the flash of the knife a second before he plunged it into her grandfather's chest. "No, old man," he repeated, "I don't need *you* anymore."

They all remained frozen while Mondry watched the life leave her grandfather's eyes. He waited a beat more, and then slowly pulled the bloody knife from her grandfather's chest. Anya knew that she would be next.

Suddenly, the doors flew open behind her. "General, we need to…." The voice ran out as he took in the scene before him.

"Yes, Hobbs?" Mondry calmly asked. He then slowly cleaned his knife off by wiping it on the shoulder of her grandfather's uniform, leaving two streaks of bright red blood behind.

Anya turned to see a small, frail-looking man. His eyes were open wide in shock, and his face had lost all color. He looked as if he were ready to faint or cry. Behind him stood the scout who had given her the lump on the side of her head. He did not look nearly as shocked as the first man. In fact, the scout looked rather bored with the whole thing.

"What have you…" Hobbs began.

Mondry looked down at the body of her grandfather as if to ask, *What? This?* He shrugged and said simply, "He'd outlived his usefulness." After a slight pause to let that sink in, he asked, "Was there a reason we were interrupted, Hobbs?"

Hobbs gave himself a small shake and seemed to come to a decision, "Yes. Yes, Sir. I just got word that the authorities are on their way. I was going to tell..." His voice faded off as he looked at the general's slumped form. He cleared his throat and continued, "I was coming to say we needed to leave right away."

"Right." Mondry said. "Gather everything that is of any importance. We leave in two minutes." Hobbs ran off to do his new master's bidding. Mondry looked down at The General's body. Something must have caught his eye, because he paused long enough to reach over and twist off the ornate ring that her grandfather wore. He studied it and then deliberately placed it on his own finger.

Mondry finally turned his attention to Anya. "Well, *princess*," he sneered, "it looks like I won't have the honor of reuniting you with your esteemed ancestry. Don't worry though, you will see them momentarily."

Before Anya could figure out what he meant, Mondry strode toward the door. As he passed the scout, he paused briefly and said, "Kill her."

"Why should I?" the scout asked.

"Because you now work for me," he said simply. He waited for the scout's nod and then walked off into the night.

CHAPTER 49

Max

Max didn't care who heard him as he kicked the front door open. He was ready for whatever met them. He was slightly surprised to not see anyone, though. From the back of the house they heard muffled yelling, followed by a loud bang. He and Koen ran in that direction.

"Anya!" he called out.

They reached the back of the house and were just in time to see two figures running through the back garden and to the street beyond. As they passed under a light, Max could see one of them had bright golden hair - Mondry.

"You find Anya," Conley said as he opened the door. "I'm going after him."

"Conley,-" Max said.

"I know what I'm doing," Conley cut in. "I will be careful," he said as he ran out to follow Mondry.

Max looked at Koen and they both rushed down the hallway to the right. "Anya!" he called again. As they drew closer to the end, they saw that the hallway stopped at a room with double doors that stood open. In the middle of the room he could see Anya tied to a chair with her back facing them. It was a relief to see she was moving, trying desperately to free herself from the bonds that held her.

He didn't think of anything other than getting to her. He rushed forward. "Dad! Don't....he's..." Her words registered too late. He was partway into the room when he saw a flash to his right. He wasn't ready for it and waited for the pain that was sure to come.

Suddenly, he was pushed from behind. He hit the floor with a thud and heard a groan behind him. Somewhere, it registered that the sound of pain had come from Koen. Max quickly flipped over to be ready for another attack. It came quickly. He saw the man come at him from above, swinging the knife down towards his chest. At the last moment he rolled to the side and brought his leg up to kick the knife out of his opponent's hand. The knife went flying, but Max knew the threat wasn't over.

He used the couch to his left for leverage to stand. Seeing the brass lamp on the adjacent table, he made a grab for it, but was spun around before he could grasp it. The punch to his gut had him doubling over in pain.

"I told you," he heard directly before pain blasted through his jaw from another explosive punch. "You should have killed me when you had the chance."

Max felt his head being pulled back by his hair. His eye was starting to swell, but he could see the face in front of him now. His brain registered that it was the scout, right before he got a fist to the face that he was sure broke his nose. Max was now dazed and sitting on the floor with his back up against the couch.

"You should never have left your enemy alive," the scout said as he put his hands around Max's neck and started to squeeze. "*I* will not be so foolish." Max felt his windpipe close as he struggled to pull the scout's hands away. His vision began to get spotty and he knew that he was only seconds away from losing consciousness. He saw a movement out of the corner of his eye. Maybe Anya had broken free and was able to get out of harm's way. His last coherent thought was the hope that she might somehow survive the night.

CHAPTER 50

Anya

As soon as the commotion had erupted, Anya had used the distraction to tip her chair over. She landed with a heavy thud on her left shoulder. She knew there would be a mighty bruise, but she had to think past the pain. As soon as the chair was on its side, she was able to slip the ropes that tied her feet to the chair off the bottom of the legs.

Once she could stand, she turned to see what was happening. She gasped as she saw her father on the floor and the scout bringing the knife down to his chest. In a flash though, her father had kicked the knife away and was getting up.

Anya took her opportunity and ran after the knife. She found it and began desperately sawing at the ropes that bound her hands. It was awkward, difficult, and far too easy to cut her hands. Soon, the blood from the cuts began to soak the ropes, but she kept cutting. Her desperation helped her feel no pain. She heard more fighting in the background, but knew she needed to concentrate on what she was doing.

Finally, her hands were free. She gripped the knife and rushed to where the scout now stood over her father. She saw her father's bloodied face and that the scout's hands were choking the life out of him. She reacted instinctively, and brought the knife down with both hands.

The scout immediately let go of her father, and turned on her with a roar. He was able to backhand her to the floor before she could duck. She expected another blow, but not feeling any, she looked up to see the scout removing the knife from between his shoulder blades. He held the knife as he stalked her. "I should have taken care of you first," he growled.

Not able to take her eyes off the knife in his hand, Anya scrambled backwards. Her back hit the desk, halting her escape. A slow smile spread across his face as he realized her predicament. "You have caused me far too much trouble, young lady," he said as he grabbed her ankle and tugged her forward. "It's time to end it." As he swung the knife down in an arch, Anya instinctively brought her arm up in defense and squeezed her eyes closed.

Suddenly, Anya heard a great thud, followed by a grunt. She opened her eyes as a heavy weight fell across her. She looked down in confusion to see the scout pinning her legs to the floor. Her eyes flew up to see Koen, swaying slightly. She watched him drop the heavy brass lamp he'd used to hit the scout and then close his eyes briefly.

Realizing that Koen was a hair's breath away from toppling over himself, she quickly scrambled out from under the scout, and moved to help him. She wedged her shoulder underneath his arm and put both of her arms around his waist.

"Ugh, my head.." he said faintly.

"I've got you," Anya told him.

"We need to leave," came her father's raspy voice.

Anya looked to see her father standing in front of them. She wasn't sure who looked worse, Koen or him. His face was bloody and bruised, and she could clearly see the welts and bruises forming around his neck. She knew that his throat had to be killing him. She nodded and he spun around to lead them out of the house.

Just then, she heard a commotion in the hallway. She noticed that her father had heard it too, because he looked back at her and Koen. She could only imagine how they looked. Her father had to know they were in no shape to fight their way out of here. He quietly positioned himself closer to her, and reached down to grab the knife that lay on the floor next to the scout. Anya could feel Koen try to rally himself to stand on his own.

All at once, the doorway was filled with armed soldiers. Anya didn't have trouble imagining what they were thinking as they looked at them and the carnage in the room.

The soldiers parted to let an older man through, the one that was obviously in charge. He first took a long look at the three of them. Then, he slowly scanned the room, not missing a detail.

"Where is Councilman Fitzgerald?" the officer demanded.

"Conley," her father began. He swallowed, cleared his throat, and tried again, "Conley went after Mondry." At the soldier's nod, her father continued, "Out the back door."

The officer made some sort of hand motion to the soldiers behind him, and several of them immediately turned around and went back the way they had come. Anya could only presume they were going to find the missing councilman. He turned to the others behind him and ordered, "Get the medics in here."

At his words, Anya suddenly began to shake. She felt Koen's arm tighten around her shoulders; he was now the one giving *her* support. The adrenaline that had kept her going suddenly evaporated, leaving exhaustion in its wake.

CHAPTER 51

Conley

Conley was thankful for the streetlights, which enabled him to keep an eye on Mondry as he ran through the streets. At the corner, Mondry and his companion had separated. There was no question who Conley would follow.

Mondry had turned right around the corner, into a darker alleyway. Conley could tell that he was headed towards the center of the city, presumably hoping to get lost among the crowds. Conley watched as Mondry took a sharp left up ahead. He was running as fast as he could, and didn't know how much longer he would be able to keep up. Taking the corner at full speed, made it impossible for Conley to stop himself when he finally saw the metal pipe coming towards him.

Mondry had been waiting for him; as soon as Conley rounded the corner, Mondry swung a pipe at him, hitting him square in the gut and causing him to land on his back in the middle of the deserted street.

Conley's breath had been knocked from him, and before he could get it back, Mondry appeared.

Mondry stood above him with his knife drawn. "You stupid old man," he admonished Conley. "Did you really think that you could catch me? Did you really think you would win -- against *me*?" With that he leaned forward and plunged his knife into Conley's gut.

Conley felt pain as he never had before.

Mondry leaned closer, "I wish you could be around to see me defeat them all, but," and here he gave the knife a vicious twist, “such is life, right?”

Conley registered Mondry’s sadistic smile, before Mondry pulled the knife out of his stomach and ran down the street.

Conley brought his hands to the wound in his stomach. He knew he was losing a lot of blood and would most likely bleed out before anyone found him. That was his last thought before everything went black.

CHAPTER 52

Anya

Anya sighed and decided that she might as well get up, since it wasn't likely she would be falling back to sleep. It was the early hours of the morning, and as she swung her feet over the side of the bed, she could see that the city outside had yet to wake. She rose and walked towards the large picture window that looked out onto The Capital City, thinking about the past two days.

It had been clear to the medical team that Captain Hawkins had requested, that Anya, Max, and Koen had needed to go to The Medical Center to treat their injuries. Captain Hawkins had sent them on their way, with several soldiers.

Even now, Anya still wasn't sure if those soldiers were for their protection, or to make sure they didn't go anywhere else.

At The Medical Center, both Koen and her father had flatly refused to be separated from Anya. The staff hadn't been quite sure what to do about that. Both of them had looked a bit menacing after the night they'd had, and Anya could tell that no one wanted to argue with them. So, with a bit of finagling, they had found a room large enough to treat all three of them at once.

Before long, Captain Hawkins had entered their room. She remembered that the medical team had seemed anxious at seeing him, so they finished quickly and left, shutting the door firmly behind them.

Once they had been alone, Anya's father spoke up,

"We will tell you everything, which will later be confirmed by Conley, but the rest of The Council needs to be here in order to hear what we have to say."

Captain Hawkins had bristled, "If you think that I'm going to bring The Council here, without even knowing—"

"Anya," her father had interrupted, "show him your shoulder."

Anya had hesitated. She remembered father looking at her and nodding. She'd slowly unbuttoned her shirt just enough to push it back, revealing her right shoulder blade. She then had turned slightly to present her back to the captain; she had heard his sudden intake of breath, then the door shutting as he left without a word.

At Anya's questioning look, her father had nodded once again. She had no idea how he could stay so calm. Between the lack of sleep and the shock of what had happened, she had felt ready to break into a million pieces.

Presently, Captain Hawkins had returned. "We are transferring you to the medic's conference room. You will be more comfortable there, and once The Council gets here, we can begin."

They had been taken to a room that doubled as a meeting room and a place the staff could eat their meals. They must have just cleared the room for them, because the spicy smell of someone's recent meal lingered behind. Even though it had been a while since she'd eaten, the smell of food had only served to make her stomach churn.

Each of them had taken seats around one of the tables. Koen had seemed to be doing a bit better, but earlier she'd heard one of the medics use the word 'concussion' when working on him, so she kept sending worried glances his way. Every time he'd caught her staring at him, he would send her a nasty scowl. This, of course, had made her feel better because he was acting completely normal.

She remembered when the two women of The Council had come in with Captain Hawkins. She'd noticed how they both looked tired, but the older woman was clearly weary and worn out. Anya had suspected it had more to do with what was happening, and less to do with the fact that it was before dawn.

"Where's Conley?" her father had asked. They'd all seen the look that passed between Captain Hawkins and the two councilwomen.

Captain Hawkins had cleared his throat, "Councilman Fitzgerald was found in an alley way."

Anya had seen her father sit up quickly, and then had heard his intake of breath at the pain the sudden movement had caused.

"He is alive," the captain continued, "but critical. They doubt he will survive the next twenty-four hours."

After a moment, her father had begun to tell them the events of the last week. She and Koen had added to the story when necessary.

When they'd finished, Karis, as she'd asked them to call her, stood and instructed Captain Hawkins to escort them to the visiting dignitary's suite.

After they'd stood up to leave, Karis had walked over to Anya and had taken a moment to study her. "You have had much thrust upon you, my dear. More experienced people than you have not been able to deal with half as much as you have. You are brave and you are stronger than you know. Hold on to that."

Anya sighed and wrapped her arms around her

middle. Now, in the dim light of morning she began to wonder. Was she? Was she really strong enough to handle all of this? She still had no idea *why* she had been the one that was chosen. She felt so *ordinary.* Wouldn't someone who had grown up in the city, someone who knew something, *anything,* about life here be better suited to the task before her?

Her thoughts were interrupted by a knock at the door. She walked across the plush carpet and into the sitting room beyond. She opened the door to find her father standing there. If it was possible, he looked even worse than he had the other night when they'd gotten here.

"I thought you would be awake too," he said as she invited him in. He brought with him a large bag, which he set on the floor next to the couch. He then walked over to the small kitchenette.

Anya sat down on one of the side chairs and closed her eyes. She could almost imagine they were back in The Outlands, and this was any ordinary morning.

"Tired?" she heard her father ask.

She opened her eyes to see him standing before her with a cup of freshly-brewed tea. She reached for it and shook her head. She wrapped her hands around the mug, reveling in the warmth and letting it seep into her.

"No," she finally said. "Dad? What happens now?"

He sat down on the small couch opposite her and looked at her with a sober expression. "I don't know, Anya," he said, shaking his head. "I just don't know. Whatever it is though, you need to know you are not alone."

Anya simply nodded, taking little comfort in his words.

Her father sighed and rose to his feet. "This was delivered for you this morning," he said as he reached for the bag he'd brought with him. "I'm guessing it's new clothes for your meeting."

Ah, yes, her meeting. She'd gotten a note yesterday, requesting her presence in something called "The Secure Chambers." Her eyes looked to the clock on the wall. They would be here soon to get her, so she stood up from the chair and took the bag her father was holding.

"Well, do you think there's anything pink in here?" she asked with feigned hopefulness.

She watched her dad smile. He kissed her on the forehead and replied, "Only if you're lucky."

She made sure he saw her exaggerated eye-roll before she turned and headed to the bathroom to get ready for the day.

CHAPTER 53

Max

Max sat next to Conley's bed. After he'd visited Anya that morning he'd headed to The Medical Center to sit with Conley. He looked at his friend, attached to a tangle of wires and tubes, and marveled once again that he was even alive. It was pure chance that they'd found him at all. A group of partiers had been heading home after a long day of celebrating in the city's center. Lucky for Conley, they'd chosen to take a shortcut through the alley where Mondry had left him. Even better, one had been a medical trainee. While the others went to get help, she had kept her wits about her and worked at stanching the flow of blood from Conley's wounds. It is because of her quick thinking that they weren't spending the day planning a state funeral. Conley hadn't woken up, but it was a testament to his enormous will that he had held on this long.

The newspaper that was lying on Conley's bedside table momentarily distracted Max. He reached for it and saw a large picture of Mondry on the front page, with the headline, "Saintly or Sinister?" For now, the official story that had been given out to the public was that Mondry had lied about being The Chosen, and when he'd been discovered, he'd attacked Councilman Fitzgerald. Apparently, there was much speculation, if the article was anything to go by. Some were theorizing that The Council had been involved all along, while others, painted Mondry as the evil mastermind who was responsible for Councilman Wilcox's death, as well as Conley's injuries.

What concerned Max was that he was sure they

had not seen the last of Mondry. There was a divide in the city, one that went back decades and just seemed to widen since he'd last been there. Mondry had hit a nerve. He had spoken of the very real disparity between those who were in powerful positions, and those who were not. Max had the feeling that there were plenty in the city who would support Mondry, even once the whole story was fully revealed. For now though, Mondry had gone underground.

As he shifted to return the newspaper, Max saw a small piece of folded paper lying on the table. He reached for it and opened it. As soon as he saw what was written on the paper, he remembered the page that Conley had torn from the book in his library. In the confusion of the last two days, Max had forgotten all about it. It must have been in one of Conley's pockets when they brought him to the hospital.

At the top of the page Max saw a picture of the symbol that he'd described to Conley. Next to the symbol were the words, "The Royal Seal of Margrave." Of course. Max recalled Anya saying something about her grandfather's ramblings, about how he had traced his lineage to Margrave, the older son of the king who had made the original deal with the Spirit. The knowledge that he was a direct descendant to the throne, must have added fuel to the fire of Mara's father's thirst for power.

"Time for your bath, Councilman."

Max turned to see a staff member wheel a cart into the room.

"Oh, I'm sorry," he said as soon as he saw Max. "I can come back..."

"No," Max said rising to his feet. "No, I was just

leaving." Max turned to Conley, and patting his hand said, "I'll be back this afternoon." Max waited a moment to see if there was any response from Conley. Seeing none, he turned and left the room.

He hadn't even made it to the elevator before the alarms began to sound. Max paused, knowing something was very wrong. He watched as medics began to run towards Conley's room. He found himself following them before he realized what he was doing. Running into the room, he bumped into the staff member who had come in to give Conley his bath. Not pausing to apologize, Max rushed to the foot of Conley's bed.

He saw a team of medics surrounding Conley's still form. It was clear to Max that in the minutes since he'd left the room, Conley's heart had stopped. This was not right. Max knew he'd left a critical, but peaceful Conley behind. Max's eyes darted around the room, desperately searching for a reason for Conley's sudden change.

His gaze landed on a lone cart in the corner of the room. It was the cart that the staff member had pushed in right before Max left. Looking at it now, Max realized that it wasn't a bath cart, but a food cart instead. Something else caught his eye. Max walked to the cart and was horrified to see a used syringe lying next to a heavy gold signet ring, a ring bearing the Seal of Margrave.

"No," Max whispered. "No, stop him!" he yelled as he rushed from of the room. He turned to run down the hall in the direction he'd seen the mysterious staff member go. All the while he knew that he was too late. Mondry had accomplished his task and would be far from The Medical Center by now.

CHAPTER 54

Anya

The loose fitting tunic and pants she'd found in the bag had pleasantly surprised Anya. Not only were they comfortable; neither of them was pink. She was ready early for her meeting, so she opened her door, thinking she could find her own way there.

As soon as she opened the door, she saw Koen come swiftly to his feet. She paused, knowing that he had been sitting in a chair outside her room. "You know," she said, "you don't have to guard me. I'm safe here."

He shot her a look that told her he didn't believe her words. If she was completely honest, she wasn't sure she believed them either. He hadn't said anything, but she suspected that it bothered him that the scout had gotten to her while she was with him in the market. No one blamed him, least of all her, but she knew that wouldn't matter to him.

His eyes scanned her appearance. His appraisal made her nervous and she had to fight against fidgeting. She wondered if he saw the same scared girl that she saw when she looked at herself in the mirror.

"Where are you going?" he asked.

"I have been invited to meet with Karis and Breanna in The Secure Chambers," Anya answered.

"I will accompany you," he said. It wasn't a request. It was a statement.

She knew that even if she told him it wasn't necessary, he would still follow her. She shrugged and turned to walk down the hallway.

They walked silently for a few minutes. It reminded Anya of the many days they had trekked through the forest on their way to The Capital City. Most of the time they never spoke a word, but Anya had eventually found a peacefulness in their silence. Now, she could feel a calm settling her frayed nerves. She realized that it was comforting just to have Koen close.

"You realize I have no idea where I am going, don't you?" Anya eventually asked.

"Yes," Koen responded.

Anya waited for more, but he simply kept walking calmly beside her. She felt her first smile in days start to bloom. "Maybe we should ask someone," she finally said.

"Maybe," he said.

She looked over to see if he might be teasing her, but his face was as serious as ever. He had his hands clasped behind his back as they walked. She saw that he looked calm and relaxed, but she knew that he was acutely aware of everything going on around them. She wondered how his head was doing. "How are you feeling?" she asked.

He turned his head to look at her. For the first time she noticed the golden flecks in his eyes.

"I'm fine," he said.

She thought that would be it but he continued.

"The headaches are gone, but the lump is still tender."

She simply nodded, glad that he was healing.

Eventually, they found themselves in front of a set of double doors. Anya figured that they had arrived at their destination because two guards flanked the doors. Once the guards saw her approach, they opened the doors for her to enter. Both Anya and Koen knew that she would be the only one permitted beyond the guards.

Anya turned to Koen, not sure what to say. Before she could say anything though, Koen spoke up, "I will be waiting here to walk you back to your rooms when you are finished."

Anya paused. "I'm not sure how long we will be," she said uncertainly.

Koen nodded and moved to the wall across from the doorway. Not seeing a chair, he leaned with his back against the wall and folded his arms across his chest. The message was clear. He would wait as long as it took.

With renewed confidence, Anya stepped through the doors and walked along a carpeted hallway to the door to The Secure Chamber. She could see through the open door that Breanna and Karis were both there, getting something to drink and organizing paperwork. Anya walked to the threshold and hesitated, not sure if she was supposed to go in.

"Intimidating, isn't it?"

Anya looked up to see Breanna studying her.

She smiled a friendly smile. "I remember my first time coming here. I was still so shocked that I had received The Mark. I was just waiting for someone to tell me it had all been an impossible joke."

"We all were surprised when you showed up, Breanna," Karis said.

Anya's eyes flew to Breanna, and widened when they saw her stick her tongue out at Karis.

"Oh, stop it, Karis," Breanna shot back. "You will scare Anya away."

Karis looked up and gave Anya a measured look, "I'm sure that she does not scare as easily as that." Karis was standing behind a burgundy leather chair. She pulled out the chair and said, "Now that you are here we may begin."

Anya walked through the doorway and to the chair that Karis had pulled out for her. Before she sat, she noticed the brass plate with her name on it. That, above all else, made this all seem terribly real.

Anya sat and watched as Breanna shut and secured the door.

"Anya," she said as she sat, "this is our safe room. You are always able to speak freely here."

Anya nodded and understood. No matter what she felt, she could talk of it here. Anya couldn't help but wonder at the secrets this room held.

Before Karis could begin, the shrill ringing of the phone interrupted them. Anya saw the look that the women exchanged.

Karis slowly rose and walked to the long table against the wall where the phone sat. She cleared her throat before she picked up the receiver. "Yes?" she said. There was a long pause as she listened to the person on the other end. "Yes, of course, I understand," she continued. "I assume you understand the delicacy of the situation. We will have a formal statement from The Council within the hour. Until then, your discretion is appreciated." Then she hung up the phone.

Karis turned to them and Anya could see her face had gone white. Breanna's eyes began to well with tears, knowing what was to come. Karis walked back to her seat and said, "It seems that our first order of business as The Council will be to find our newest member." Anya was momentarily confused, until Karis continued. "Conley has succumbed to his injuries. He passed away fifteen minutes ago."

***

An hour later Anya's head was swimming. She

knew that it had been incredibly difficult for Karis and Breanna to push past their grief and continue on. It was clear that Conley had not only been their coworker, he had also been their dear friend. There were many, many questions left to answer and much that needed to be completed, but now as Anya stood at the window in her room that overlooked the city, she felt a small spark of hope. For the first time since that day in the woods when she'd first heard of The Mark and The Chosen, she felt a sense of rightness and belonging.

Slowly, a small smile began to bloom.

EPILOGUE

He took a deep breath. He loved the clean cool air and how the disappearing sun painted the sky with bright reds and deep purples. This was always the best time to be on the water, and most nights he took advantage of the fact that his brothers and sisters were busy with their evening chores. He knew that his mother was aware that he snuck out in the evening to find some peace on the water. As long as he was home in time for dinner, he knew she didn't mind.

He took another deep breath and a last lingering look at the sunset, before he set the oars back into the water and prepared to head for home. He was three strokes into his journey when the pain exploded in his shoulder. He was accustomed to the pain that comes from hard physical labor, but this was different. He felt as if his shoulder were being burned from the inside out. He doubled over and dropped his oars. His last coherent thought was that tonight he would not be home in time for dinner.

About the Author

Elizabeth Valente has been a teacher for eighteen years, teaching everything from kindergarten music, to middle school reading and writing, and more recently, Young Adult Literature at a local university. Along with writing and teaching, Elizabeth has a passion for knitting, spinning wool, and running – not necessarily in that order.

Elizabeth lives with her family in Michigan. You can connect with Elizabeth on Facebook at http://www.facebook.com/ElizabethsWriterlyWorld or Twitter @WovenOwlPub.

The Revealing
By Elizabeth Valente

CHAPTER 1

Jemma

Jemma was afraid. It wasn't the kind of fear that went away with the dawn of a new day. It was the kind of fear that went deeper, a fear that was real. It was always there in the shadows, waiting for her guard to come down. It was then that it would sneak out and whisper to her, telling her to never forget that it was still there, waiting. From the moment she'd found out she was pregnant, the fear had grown stronger each day. She'd tried to talk about it with Gareth, but no matter how much he tried to listen and sympathize, she knew that he thought it was a fear that was not grounded in reality. When she realized that the worry lines she saw on his face were there because of her, she stopped mentioning it to him at all. She put a good show on for him, but there were times when she felt overwhelmed and fragile, as if at any moment she could break into a million pieces.

Jemma paused in her cleaning and looked up to see herself in the bathroom mirror. She often wondered what others saw when they looked at her. Inevitably the first thing they noticed was her mane of wild orange hair. She'd tried and tried to tame it over the years, but it followed no rules. The curls seemed to have a life of their own and only escaped from any constraints she tried to put on them. Gareth told her that her hair was the color of the sunset, but she knew better; it was orange and it was obnoxious. She sighed as she tucked a wayward curl behind her ear. The rest of her face projected a delicacy that she hated. She wanted to be strong and to look strong, but her fair skin and the sprinkle of freckles across her pixie nose made her look more like a teenager than a grown woman. The only things that she felt really reflected who she was were her eyes. They were a deep chocolate brown and held a quiet solemnity that revealed her gentle spirit. Gareth always told her that it was her hair that had first gotten his attention, but it was her eyes that had kept it.

Jemma needed a distraction and decided a trip to the center of the city might be helpful. It was Market Day and there were sure to be plenty of diversions. She stopped cleaning and gathered her things before she could change her mind. As she closed the front door of her house, she could immediately feel herself feeling lighter. Maybe she would make Gareth's favorite meal tonight. He was working on the south section of the wall today, and she knew he would come home hungry after a long day of hauling stone.

The business of Market Day always surprised her when she first came out of the narrow street that led to the open area reserved for all the vendors. On every other day of the week the center of the city was quiet and nearly deserted at midday, but not on Market Day. The courtyard seemed to be alive with action. It wasn't only the sights and sounds that caught Jemma's attention today though; she was also struck by the smells. It seemed that with this pregnancy her sense of smell had rocketed into overdrive. Gareth had remarked that her cooking had become so much better lately, and she attributed it to the fact that she could smell spices and herbs as she never had before. She had been lucky enough to find one vender who specialized in every kind of spice and herb you could imagine. She made a mental note to stop by Luella's stall today and pick up some more ginger.

Jemma took her time walking through the stalls, enjoying the feeling of being surrounded by the others that lived in The Capital City and the surrounding villages. She liked listening to the conversations of the other women, hearing them list their mundane chores and the odd complaint about their husbands' idiosyncrasies. Sometimes she would feign interest in a particular vendor's wares, just to hear the end of a juicy tale. She and Gareth had often laughed at the stories she brought home.

"...I'm telling you Millie, it would be a huge honor."

Jemma looked up to see two women approach the pile of fruit next to the one she was looking through. She noticed that one of them was heavily pregnant, probably not much further along than she was. The other was tall, thin, and had the air of someone who liked to give out advice, even if it wasn't always welcome.

"We were lucky enough to have *two* of ours born on a Day of Power," the pregnant woman's friend told her.

Jemma felt her throat close and the fear begin to close in. She suspected that her face had gone just as white as Millie's had at the woman's words.

"We were ecstatic to head to The Center as soon as we could to hand them over. We even threw a party after the second one. Do you know how *rare* that is, to have two Storm Children?"

Jemma caught Millie's eye and saw a mirror image of the panic she herself felt. Jemma instinctively brought her hand to her protruding stomach and felt the movement of the baby within. She recognized it as the protective gesture it was. She could not lose another child, even if it was to The Center.

"Hopefully, the storm will hold off for another week, so that your child can be born during it as well. You know," the woman continued in a bit of a whisper, "there are ways to make sure the baby holds off until the Day of Power." She quickly straightened up and clarified, "Not that *I* had to resort to those, mind you, but I know a woman..." she continued on her way to the next vendor, never pausing to make sure Millie followed. With one last desperate look at Jemma, Millie hurried after the woman.

Jemma felt that the day had suddenly become dim. She had to take a few deep breaths in order to compose herself. Her mind knew that she should finish her shopping, and she had to fight against her instinct to immediately run home. She decided that the only thing she really needed was the ginger, so she put down the apple she'd been holding and hurried to Luella's stall.

It seemed that the number of shoppers had grown, and it became difficult for Jemma to easily maneuver throughout the crowded streets. Finally, sweaty and exhausted, she arrived at Luella's stall. Her panic was nearing the breaking point, so she wanted to get the ginger as quickly as possible and head for home.

"Jemma!" she heard Luella call to her. She tried to calm her features and smile. Jemma, normally very shy, had met the older woman months ago and had immediately felt a kinship with her. There was something about Luella that had drawn Jemma in. She suspected that Luella was a Seer, as well as someone who sold spices and herbs, but Jemma had never asked for information from her, even though she'd wanted to so desperately.

"Hi, Luella," she said softly. "I was just coming by to get some ginger." Jemma could see Luella looking at her with a sharp, knowing gaze. Jemma guessed that Luella was somewhere in her sixth decade, just by some of the things she'd mentioned, but she certainly didn't look it. She had thick dark hair that cascaded heavily past her shoulders and was just beginning to grow silver at her temples. Her eyes were a piercing blue that Jemma was sure saw more than some were comfortable with. Jemma suspected they never missed even the smallest detail. Luella was petite, but her personality was anything but diminutive. Jemma knew she was a force to be reckoned with, but Luella was always very gentle with her. Luella seemed to sense Jemma's innate shyness, and Jemma suspected that she dialed back her personality just a bit because of that.

"I will get the ginger packaged for you in a minute," Luella said quickly. "You just come around here and have a seat. I have some nice lavender tea all ready for you."

"Oh," Jemma said, "I can just wait here.."

"Nonsense," Luella said with a wave of her hand. "You come back here and sit down." She reached out and grabbed Jemma's hand and pulled her around the stall's display to a chair behind the counter. "You've been carrying that babe all afternoon. It's time you took a load off."

The very last thing that Jemma wanted to do was sit for a visit. She *needed* to get home, but one look at Luella told her there was no way around it; she was styaing. Before she knew what was happening, she was sitting on a comfortable chair with a cup of tea in her hand.

Jemma figured that she might as well try to distract herself from her thoughts. She wrapped both hands around the warm mug and breathed in deeply of the calming sent of lavender and peppermint. As she took her first sip, her eyes never left Luella, who seemed particularly busy today. Jemma was taken aback when she could feel the tension begin to drain from her shoulders. How had Luella known that *this* was exactly what she'd needed?

Before long the tea was gone and Luella was able to rest for a moment beside Jemma. They sat silently for a while, both enjoying the sights and sounds around them. It was as if they had found the only quiet haven amidst a busy, bustling world.

"You will find peace, you know," Luella said quietly. "You are stronger than you believe."

Jemma was startled and her eyes flew to Luella's. She instinctively brought her hand to her stomach and watched as Luella's knowing eyes caught her movement.

"May I?" Luella asked, gesturing to the mug that Jemma still held in her hand. It took Jemma a moment to realize what she was asking. Jemma looked into the empty mug and saw the spattering of tea leaves stuck to the bottom. She wasn't sure if she even believed in the ability of tea leaves to predict one's future, but she found herself handing over the mug anyway.

Luella took a moment to study the contents of the mug. "So much sadness," Luella began. "Your past is dark with it." Luella looked up at Jemma and paused before looking down at Jemma's stomach. "He is not your first."

That matter of fact statement was like a knife to the heart. No, this baby was not her first. Jemma closed her eyes and gave herself a moment to remember. She remembered her daughter's small hands. At time she'd sworn she could still feel the feather light touch of them on her cheek. She remembered her daughter's delighted giggle whenever Gareth had lifted her high into the air. She remembered the day her daughter took her first wobbly steps, how excited she'd been, and how she had regretted how quickly time was passing.

As it always was when she let herself think of those wonderful memories, they were quickly replaced by the darker ones. She remembered the first time she had known something was not right. She remembered her insistence to Gareth that they take the child to The Medical Center. She remembered the face of the doctor who had delivered the news that every parent dreads. She remembered sitting by her daughter's bedside, trying to fit a lifetime of love into every touch and cuddle. She remembered the day she'd held her daughter as the life faded from her.

Jemma opened her eyes and knew that every bit of pain she felt was reflected in them. For months she had wondered if she was strong enough to go through all of this again. When she'd realized she was pregnant, her fears and doubts had flooded in. She knew she wouldn't survive another loss. She heard again Luella's words, *you are stronger than you believe.* She wondered if she would ever believe that.

Luella reached over and gave her hand a squeeze. "He is strong, Jemma. His fate is not the same as hers."

Luella's words broke through her pain. *He?* Was it true that she carried a son? She wanted to believe that, because she wanted to believe Luella's assurances about his future even more. She watched as Luella brought her attention back to the mug she still held.

"Your present is clouded in gray," Luella said without looking up. "Fear has you in its grip. You worry about losing another child, either to sickness or to The Center." She looked up and saw the confirmation of her words on Jemma's face. "He is strong, Jemma. Much will be asked of him, and he will look to you for strength. You must begin now to push the fear away."

Jemma waited a moment, then realized that Luella was finished. She had many questions, but it wasn't in her nature to push. She needed time to digest what Luella had told her, maybe next week she would come back to Luella for more information. She gathered her things and stood.

Luella stood as well and handed her a bundled package. "Here is your ginger, and a little something extra for you. No, no," Luella said, seeing Jemma reach for money to pay her, "consider it a gift."

"Well," Jemma replied, "the next time I see you, I will bring you a special treat."

Seeing Luella hesitate, Jemma sensed she had more to say, but was struggling with how to put it.

"I will see you sooner than you may think." Before Jemma could question her she went on. "Your journey will begin soon. It will be long and difficult, but know you are strong enough to meet every challenge you will face. Follow your instincts, they will not lead you in the wrong direction." Here Luella pulled Jemma close for a fierce hug and whispered, "Have faith in yourself."

The whole way home, Jemma turned Luella's words over and over in her mind. What did she mean by a journey? Would Gareth finally give in to her urgings to leave the city before this year's Day of Power arrived? She knew that he would never leave without the assurance that there was work wherever they went. He would never leave the future of his family to the whims of fate. The thing was, The Capital City was so cut off from The Outlands, that many weren't even sure what was out there. The rumors of lawlessness and poverty were so rampant that to even suggest taking his family there was unheard of. Jemma shook her head as she opened the door to their home. Luella had told her to trust her instincts, so that's what she would have to do.

As Jemma stepped across the threshold she heard a noise in the back of the house. Fear immediately clinched her throat closed and tightened her muscles as she prepared to run back out the door she'd just come through.

"Jemma?" she heard from the back, "is that you?"

She watched as Gareth walked up the hallway, wiping the lower half of his face on a blue towel from the bathroom. Realizing it was only him, she tried to calm her racing heart. Jemma knew he must have seen the fear and surprise on her face, because his countenance immediately softened and he came quickly to her.

"Here," he said, lifting the package from her hands, "let me take that." He laid it on the table and started to lead her to a chair.

Jemma smiled and shook her head. "You scared me, you big oaf," she said teasingly. "What are you doing home so early? I wasn't gone that long."

He returned her smile while he gently pulled her into his arms. "You were gone long enough to turn into a fishwife, I see. Is that any way to greet your husband?"

Early in their marriage that question would have made her shyly apologize, but now she knew better. Now she understood that his question was not one of rebuke, but teasing. Not saying a word she raised her eyebrows and folded her arms, waiting for an answer to *her* question.

Gareth let out a hearty laugh and pulled her closer to him.

After a moment, she sighed and relaxed against him, wrapping her arms around him as best she could with her protruding middle. She had to admit, she never felt more protected and cared for than when he held her like this. Where she was small, Gareth was big. When they'd first met, she'd expected him to be clumsy, or at least brutish, but she soon found out he was neither. He had a certain grace about him, and though he was strong, he always held his strength in check. Jemma looked up a him and couldn't help but smile. Oh, how she loved his open happy face. His green eyes fairly sparkled with laughter and mischief. His ruddy face and unruly mop of blond hair made him seem even more like the impish schoolboy she was sure he'd been.

He leaned down to give her a peck on her upturned nose and then said, "I came home to help pack."

Jemma started and drew back in surprise. "Pack?" she said. "What do you mean 'pack'?"

Gareth let go of her and, with a huge smile on his face, began to explain. "I don't know why I didn't think of it earlier." At her look of impatience, he continued, "Okay, okay. You are worried about the baby being born during a Day of Power, right?" At Jemma's slow nod, he continued. "So, why don't we take a trip?"

"What are you talking about?" Jemma asked.

Gareth came in closer and put his hands on her upper arms. "What I mean is, why don't we leave the city, just until the baby is born, and then we can come back and resume our lives."

Jemma began to realize what he was suggesting and he was right; why *hadn't* they thought of this earlier?

"You see?" Gareth asked as he saw realization dawn on her face. "You only have a week, maybe two to go, right?" He waited for Jemma's nod and then continued. "I've cleared it with the foreman, I can take two weeks off and still keep my position. If we travel beyond the city walls it won't matter if there is a Day of Power, because we won't be *here* when it happens. Then, as soon as you and the baby are able, we will come back." Gareth waited a moment for his words to sink in.

Yes. Yes, *this* must be the journey that Luella had been talking about. *Follow your instincts*, she had told Jemma, and every instinct was telling her that this was a brilliant plan. This could work.

"When do we..?" Jemma began.

"I have to go to the wall tomorrow. We are closing off a hole and every hand is needed, but after that we can leave."

The worry and fear that had been building for months left her in a moment. She knew that Gareth could see that when his look of excitement mirrored her own.

"Okay," she directed, "You go pack clothing, I will work on putting food together for our journey." They both laughed and they ran to get everything ready for their journey.

***

One would think, with the day she'd had, that she would have been exhausted by the time she'd finally gotten into bed. She'd told Gareth to go off to bed hours ago. He'd protested, but she had assured him that she was fine. He needed to work in the morning, and she'd had just a few more things to gather. She'd found packets of lavender tea in the package that Luella had given her that afternoon. So, she'd brewed a cup and sipped on it as she lovingly packed some of the clothing she'd made for the baby over the last few months. She'd known that she couldn't bring all of it, so she had sorted through what she thought the baby might need, focusing on what would keep him warm and comfortable.

Now, Jemma smiled as she climbed into bed next to her snoring husband. She took a moment to search her heart for the fear that had become so familiar, but she only found joy and peace. She could feel her limbs relaxing, getting ready for sleep. Even the baby, who normally chose bedtime to be active, was peacefully quiet. She closed her eyes and began to drift off to sleep.

She came awake suddenly, at first not sure what was happening. She didn't know if she'd just closed her eyes, or if it had been hours since she'd come to bed, but as soon as the second pain hit, it didn't matter. She gasped for breath and instinctively grabbed for Gareth, who sat up suddenly. She could tell that he was disoriented and could hear him fumbling in the dark to turn on the light.

The light came on suddenly. She could only imagine what he saw. She was now doubled over, holding her stomach, feeling her muscles tightening with the contraction she was experiencing. Once it had passed she looked up at his stunned face.

"Now?" was his whispered question.

Jemma nodded and said, "Now," right before the next contraction stole her breath. It was as her muscles were beginning to relax again that the first crash of lightening hit the city.

CHAPTER 2

Josiah

16 Years Later

He made sure to approach the door with caution, for what awaited him on the other side was not certain. He paused for a moment to place his ear against the rough wood. Maybe, if he were extremely still, he would hear something that would give him a clue. He listened for a moment, but other than the soft whinny of a horse, he heard nothing. He closed his eyes and took a deep breath. He focused all his energy on what was contained inside the building he was about to enter.

He had always had the ability to feel what those around him were feeling, almost as if they were his own emotions. It had begun when he was young. He'd never known he was different; he'd always assumed that everyone was connected in the way he was. It wasn't until his father had brought him to the town's market on butchering day that it became clear no one else was like him.

Josiah could still remember that day vividly. He hadn't been much more than six years old and his mother being busy at home, had sent he and his father to get supplies. He remembered that the trip had started out wonderfully. His father had treated them both to a special treat of sweet bread, but only after Josiah had promised not to tell his mother. For some reason, she had strong feelings about sweets before dinner. They'd laughed as they had licked their fingers clean, getting rid of any evidence. The last stop they'd needed to make was to the butcher, to get the pork that his mother had wanted. They'd been calmly walking through the town's small square when Josiah had suddenly stopped and refused to go any further. He'd felt a fear so strong that he could almost see it; it was a sickening red that rolled over him in waves. The fear had come from the far end of the village, where the butcher was located.

Josiah hadn't known what was happening to him at the time, but now he knew it was the terror of the animals being butchered that he was feeling.

His father hadn't understood Josiah's reaction and had tried to pick him up and carry him to get the meat they'd needed, but he had fought like a wildcat. Eventually, his father had just turned around, brought Josiah home to his mother, and then went back to town for the pork.

It had been Josiah's mother who had finally figured out what had turned her normally obedient and amiable child into a hysterical hellion. That night, she'd placed a piece of pork on his plate for dinner and watched, stunned, as silent tears rolled down his face.

For the first time he knew where his food came from, and the horror those animals experienced in order to feed him. He couldn't eat it.

After dinner, his mother had taken him for a walk down by the pier. It was while they'd been sitting on a dock, dipping their toes in the salty water and watching the sunset, that he'd been able to tell her about what he'd felt that day.

He remembered asking her how everyone else could ignore what those animals were feeling. That's when he'd learned that not everyone felt as deeply as he did. It was then that he'd learned he was different. His mother had told him he was "special," that his ability was "a gift," but he wasn't so sure he believed that. How could sharing someone's terror and pain be a gift?

From that day on he was never expected to go to the village on butchering days or to eat meat, for that matter. He loved both of his parents for never making an issue of either of those things.

Now, he stood outside the barn and could feel the nervous energy of the animals within. They were not comfortable with whatever was happening inside. They were anxious and overwhelmed, not a good combination when one of them was getting ready to foal. Knowing that now was the time to act, he reached down for the door handle. As he gripped the rusted iron, he suddenly felt a sharp hint of excited anticipation wash over him. Again, these emotions were not his own. He knew he was feeling the emotions of the others inside the barn. It was clear that they knew someone was looking for them, and they didn't have long to remain hidden.

Josiah pulled the door slowly outward, wanting to minimize any noise. He gave his eyes a moment to adjust to the darkness within and then carefully stepped inside. He tried to focus on the feelings of excitement he'd felt moments ago, hoping to be able to pinpoint their origin, but a sudden loud squeal from above startled him. He caught sight of the falling object and reacted instinctively. He put out his arms and ran the two steps necessary for him to catch the precious cargo that fell from the loft above.

"Jo-Jo find me! Jo-Jo find me!" his little sister yelled. He looked down at the giggling three year old he held in his arms and tried to calm his racing heart.

Before he could say anything he heard a sound of frustration coming from a pile of hay near the horses' stalls.

Moments later an angry six year old boy with a curly mop of bright orange hair, stood up and yelled, "I told you we shouldn't have let her play with us!"

"What was I supposed to do?" came the irritated retort from across the barn. "It was either let her play, or have her give us away!" An exact replica of the first boy came stomping across the hay and met his brother face to face in front of Josiah. Nose to nose those two stood, ready to battle it out.

"Well, that's what she did anyway!" said the first boy.

By now Josiah had gotten his heartbeat under control and he knew if he didn't step in soon, he would be breaking up a brawl between the twins. Since Emmie had now latched onto his neck, and it didn't look like she would be letting go any time soon, Josiah took a step forward to put himself between his brothers.

"Look guys, why don't we play tomorrow, just the three of us?" Before they could open their mouths to whine about Emmie getting involved then too, Josiah leaned down and said softly, "We'll play while she takes her nap." Josiah watched a new gleam enter their identical pairs of green eyes.

The twins looked at each other, and without a word ran out of the barn, presumably to plan tomorrow's hiding strategy.

Josiah shook his head and knelt down on one knee, putting his little sister's feet on the floor in the process. He gently removed her arms from around his neck and looked down at her upturned face. Oh, how he loved this little one. She, out of all his siblings, was the only one who had inherited the exuberant joy that was such a part of their father, as well as the chocolate brown eyes and curly red hair of their mother. He also knew that she was especially sensitive, so he took a moment, wanting to be careful how he phrased what he needed to tell her.

"Emmie?" he asked.

"Yes, Jo-Jo?" She smiled up at him, but the serious look she saw made her realize this was not a time for teasing and fun.

Josiah watched her brown eyes grow huge and worried. "Emmie, remember how I told you not to go up into the loft?" At her nod, he continued. "What if I hadn't caught you when you fell?"

"But Jo-Jo did," she said innocently.

"But what if I hadn't?" he insisted.

Her eyes began to fill with tears, but he knew it wasn't because she was thinking about the possibility of getting hurt. He understood that she was afraid he was angry with her. He took a deep breath and steeled himself against the urge to tell her it was all right. He knew there might come a day when he wouldn't be there to catch her, and the thought of her getting hurt was too much for him to bear.

"Emmie, you *have* to promise that you won't go up to the loft." By now she had dropped her head, so he put his knuckle under her chin to lift up her face. "Promise me, Emmie."

Emmie gave a little hiccup and whispered, "I promise."

"Good," Josiah said. "Where's Rana? Wasn't she supposed to be watching you?" He watched Emmie look up to the loft and shrug. Josiah guessed that Rana had gotten distracted with her drawings, and seeing an opportunity, Emmie had made a run for it. Josiah nodded, "Okay, Mom wants you inside for your lessons, so run along now while I check on the horses."

Before he could get to his feet, Emmie threw her arms around his neck. He gave her a squeeze in return and she planted a sloppy kiss on his cheek. He couldn't help but smile and he was happy to hear her giggling as she ran out the door.

Josiah figured that the horses could wait a few more minutes, so he turned and began climbing the wooden ladder that led to the barn's loft. He reached the top easily and paused for a moment to look over his shoulder to the barn floor below. He shuttered at the thought of Emmie launching herself off the edge, trusting in him to catch her. She would be the end of him, he was sure.

He pulled himself up the rest of the way and began walking to the far corner of the loft, knowing that was mostly likely where he would find Rana. He spotted her tucked next to one of the thin windows that provided light and ventilation to the barn. As he'd expected, she was completely focused on what she was doing.

Rana had her large sketchpad propped up on her bent knees, as her gaze toggled between the page she was working on and something outside in the yard. Today she was working with bits of charcoal, which she'd probably pilfered from the supply in the kitchen. Her hands were caked in black dust as she alternated between sketching and blending her drawing.

Josiah watched as Rana lifted her hand and impatiently swiped at a long blond curl that was tickling her face. He chuckled softly and shook his head at the dark streak she'd left behind on her cheek.

People often assumed that Rana was vain and selfish. Her looks and natural reticence made her seem so, but those who really knew her, understood that was far from the truth. At thirteen, she was a beautiful girl with long wheat colored hair and bright green eyes. She had inherited their mother's delicate features and quiet manor, and like her mother, she much preferred standing in the background, rather than being the one who was receiving any attention. Josiah knew that her looks would not allow that of her as she grew older. Other girls her age were just beginning to understand their power over the boys of the village, but the only thing Rana ever really focused on was her drawings. She was too busy drinking in the world around her so she could recreate it later in her notebook. Josiah had seen the boys follow her when she went to town, and knew that part of her attraction was the fact that she was completely unaware of them.

Josiah quietly moved toward Rana. As the roof sloped downward, he needed to hunch over until eventually he was crawling on all fours. He sat down next to her and looked over her shoulder at what she was doing.

The subject of Rana's drawing was the ebony stallion their father had recently brought home. She'd drawn him mid-leap and had somehow perfectly captured his power and defiance.

"I just can't get his hind legs right," Rana muttered with a hint of frustration.

Josiah thought they looked perfectly fine, but he also knew that Rana wouldn't listen to any reassurances from him. "You will get it just how you want it," he said. "Keep practicing."

Rana finally turned and smiled softly at him, happy with his simple confidence in her. She then looked beyond his shoulder as she fully came out of her artistic stupor. Her smile fell when she realized that there were no sounds of children playing. "I did it again, didn't I?"

Josiah nodded. He knew she felt badly about not keeping a close eye on the little ones, but he also understood that she didn't intentionally lose track of time and space when she was drawing. He didn't know what the solution was, so he just sighed and motioned towards the house. "Mom sent me out to find all of you. It's time for lessons."

Rana's shoulders slumped even further, as she moved to gather her things.

He knew how much she hated the structure and tedium of her daily lessons. "Hey," he said, "why don't you gather up your things here and maybe after supper you can come with me for a boat ride."

Rana's face immediately brightened. He suspected it wasn't the company she was excited about, but the possibility of basking in the colors of the sunset that she was anticipating. She quickly finished packing up her things and scrambled over to the ladder.

"You might want to wash up before you head in," he called to her. He laughed as she rolled her eyes and let out a groan. He knew she would be perfectly content living with her smudged fingers, but they both knew their mother would not.

Josiah followed his sister's path and began lowering himself down the ladder. He actually did need to check on the mare. He suspected that it would be any day now that she would have her foal and they needed to have everything ready to help her. As he continued down the ladder, he nearly missed the last rung because of an unexpected pain in his shoulder. He righted himself quickly and stepped down to the floor of the barn. He gingerly gave his right shoulder an experimental roll, while mentally questioning what he might have done to it. The pain lingered for a moment, but then was gone, leaving a slight ache in its place. He shook his head. He must have done something to his shoulder when he caught Emmie. He absently wondered if his mother had any ointments or herbs for muscle pain as he began walking towards the horses' stalls.

Book 2 of *The Marked Series,*

The Revealing

Coming summer of 2016

Made in the USA
Middletown, DE
23 May 2016